A DAY AT THE RACES

A DAY AT THE RACES

Frances Paige

This first world edition published in Great Britain 2002 by
SEVERN HOUSE PUBLISHERS LTD of
9–15 High Street, Sutton, Surrey SM1 1DF.
This first world edition published in the USA 2003 by
SEVERN HOUSE PUBLISHERS INC of
595 Madison Avenue, New York, N.Y. 10022.

British Library Cataloguing in Publication Data

Paige, Frances
    A day at the races
    1.   Women in horse racing - France - Fiction
    2.   Irish - France - Fiction
    3.   Love stories
    I.   Title
    823.9'14 [F]

    ISBN 0-7278-5900-5

Typeset by Hewer Text Ltd.,
Edinburgh, Scotland.
Printed and bound in Great Britain by
MPG Books Ltd., Bodmin, Cornwall.

One

P addy would have been pleased, Nora thought, going into the travel shop opposite the Tuileries. Six months since he'd died, and he was still with her, a mental yardstick for everything she did. Strange to be a trainer, as he had been, and have a daughter who didn't share his passion for horses. 'Oh, I like them,' she'd said, 'but I'm not *mad* about them like you.'

'I blame your mother,' he'd said once. 'Couldn't bear the smell of good horse dung.'

'Papa, *la crotte*,' she'd said, teasing him, '*s'il te plaît.*' That's how they'd been. An easy relationship . . .

'I'd like to book an all-in ticket for the races at Chantilly,' she said to the clerk behind the counter. In perfect French.

He was appreciative. He could offer a select coach, entry tickets, a small picnic hamper, '*Dîner sur l'herbe*,' he joked, '*champagne, foie gras.*'

She said that was very suitable. Again in perfect French.

In the coach she didn't fraternize at first, only dimly aware of the other occupants. Not many: two young couples, an elderly woman with a youngish man, a courier. Too expensive for some. She closed her eyes . . .

She had tried her best to fill her mother's place when she had so suddenly deserted them. Although she was only ten at

1

the time, she was old enough to hear and understand the gossip in the yard, the hidden laughter, that Mrs Laure Malone, the boss's wife, had taken off with his manager, a smart alec but handsome young man of twenty-three.

Her sympathies had all been with her father, her ears had burned for him, so loving, patient, so good-humoured. On the other hand, she had never known where she was with her mother, a creature of moods, sometimes waltzing her around the house, laughing, singing, at other times throwing herself on her bed in tears. 'I can't stand it any more! I have to get away . . .'

Mother had been French, of course, and early on she had insisted on Nora being entered for Ste-Catherine's, an old-fashioned seminary, now in Paris, which she herself had attended. 'You've got to be taught deportment, how to use your hands, *comme ça*, how to wear your clothes. How do you think you will ever comport yourself in society, attract men?' It hadn't occurred to her. She was quite content with Paddy and the peace they enjoyed together. Without mother.

It was on her first end-of-term holiday from Paris that she began to call her father Paddy not Papa. Her role, as she saw it, now that she was a young lady of sixteen, was to look after him, occasionally help in the office and to accompany him to race meetings. Although she didn't see it, he had become the most important person in her life.

She had boyfriends, not surprisingly with her colouring, glossy brown hair, long legs, a high-held head (difficult not to use equine terms if you live in the ambience), and a complexion which could only be likened to the cream which was sometimes fed to a new-born foal. Those young men who buzzed around the paddock and loose boxes and had never received what they hoped for – an invitation to the old stone house with the colonial pillars – reluctantly transferred

2

their attentions to the thoroughbreds which Paddy was training.

Her love for her father probably explained why, in 1985, when she was nineteen and in her last year at Ste-Catherine's, she was still a virgin. In spite of Madame de Reignier's strict régime, there were always a few adventurous girls who escaped it. And where better than in a city devoted to *l'amour* . . .

At this point Nora left her reverie and glanced out of the coach window at the stream of traffic of all kinds: chara-bancs, closed cars, open cars, some occupants wearing period dress, top hats, flower-trimmed hats; everyone off to enjoy the race meeting . . . Had it been like that on the day Paddy remembered so well? 1962. 'Do it for me, Nora, will you?' And she had promised . . .

And there was Liam, it seemed there had always been Liam, whose mother, Mhairi, was housekeeper at March-mount. Liam who had grown up with Nora, had schooled her for the point-to-points, and who now put down her reserve to a lack of curiosity. He didn't go further than that, but what he meant was sex; not overt sex, but all the delicious and natural overtures and more between young men and women.

'There's a whole world out there,' he'd told her once, but hadn't said he thought her extreme devotion to Paddy was unusual in a young nubile girl, not to mention, unhealthy.

Although he was now studying to be a land surveyor, his childhood trailing about the yard after his father, a jockey of such excellence that he'd been on a retainer to Paddy, had coloured his outlook and given him a natural way of looking at things.

Nora's grandfather, Colonel Maguire of nearby Lisbor-ough House, never seemed to have got over his daughter's defection from Paddy and her young daughter. He tended to

3

be distant with Nora, but Paddy said she had to try to understand what a bitter blow it had been for him. 'And don't toss your head like a flighty filly,' he'd said, making her laugh. She had admitted to herself that for some time after her mother had left them, she had resented Grandfather's frequent visits to Marchmount where he and Paddy closeted themselves in the study with a bottle of whiskey. 'Eddie's had damned bad luck,' he had said. 'One day you'll know all about it.'

Why all the secrecy, she'd thought. Typical of men.

Everybody adored Paddy. Mhairi, who was everlastingly grateful to him, would say, 'I won't hear a thing against Paddy.' She had a straight back and bold eyes. 'To take me on here when my Seumus was thrown and killed by that bad-eyed brute at Leopardstown . . . He's a saint!'

'Well, it's a pity that your Liam decided to leave him in the lurch and become a land surveyor!' Nora'd said. 'Paddy depended on him.'

'Ah, well, Liam. That one is a law unto himself.'

Nora sometimes thought there was a lack of rapport between Liam and his mother.

But as she grew older, and more sensible, she made a discovery because of her closeness to Paddy. Behind his good-humour, jauntiness and kindness, she thought there was a deep-seated sadness. It disturbed her, made her wonder if he still missed her mother in spite of the love she wrapped him in.

No one could look happier than he did most of the time. He was always welcoming and charming to the wealthy owners who came to see him and who were always entertained like royalty in the white-panelled dining room. The wide apron of green lawn could be seen through the long windows, stretching out to the paddock with the white fencing, the green fields beyond, and the far-off mistiness of the Wicklow mountains.

4

She had often helped Mhairi by setting the table with snowy linen, Waterford glass, and the Georgian silver (the devil to clean, Mhairi said), leaving Mhairi to prepare the dishes which the men liked: prime cuts of beef from Galway and game from the nearby Lisborough estate. Paddy often invited Grandfather as well.

He had liked Nora to act as hostess, sitting in what had been Laure's place. And he liked her in white – 'while she's still entitled to wear it,' he'd say with a laugh – and her looking like one of those tea roses in the middle of the lawn.

Mhairi saw to her culinary skills as well, and when she was teaching her to, say, make a syllabub, would chat away.

'Of course your grandfather, Colonel Maguire, was a great racing man, didn't you know? Hardly ever missed a race meeting. Abroad as well. Not immediately, when your grannie died young, poor soul. Oh, dear no, he stayed put with little Laure and saw that she had good nannies and that, but when she went to that French school you went to, he and Paddy had fine times together all over the place, although there will be twenty years or more between them. Aye, sure enough, the Colonel was game for anything, gay Paree and all that.'

'Mrs Know-all,' Nora would say.

'Well, wasn't it my Seumus who kept me informed? He was riding a neat little three-year-old in the Prix de Diane at Chantilly which Paddy said looked as if it had come out of the Cluny Museum, wherever that is . . .'

'And my mother and a friend were there too, and she knew Paddy, of course, being neighbours, and so there were wedding bells soon after . . .' She'd heard it all before.

'Not that soon. Laure and her friend were a couple of beauties, my Seumus told me, one fair, the other dark with rosy cheeks and bright eyes – that was your mother. You're not a bit like her.'

'Thank you very much.'

'And then for her to run away with that toerag, Kevin Flannagan. Oh, but what am I doing chattering away like this when I've got better things to do . . .'

There was always something left out. But why, when you came to think of it, had a woman of her mother's upbringing chosen Kevin Flannagan as her only means of escape? Particularly someone who had been at Ste-Catherine's with its emphasis on dignity and adherence to a certain standard of behaviour?

Actually, she had liked being there. She had been a good student, and her early love of medieval history, fostered by incessant reading, troubadours and the like, had been encouraged by Mademoiselle Vidalle. She had enjoyed the museums, the art galleries, the introduction to the prevailing Gothic influence of the Parisian churches and cathedrals. Her mother had been flightier, she knew, but, still, Kevin Flannagan, a stable hand really . . .

No, she and her mother were different. Laure was a Parisian, had been brought up there; she, although she liked Paris, had never stopped missing Marchmount: the leaping fires; the paddock with the sycamores on the leeward side; the bustle of the morning ride; the general greenness compared with the grey Parisian streets (silver in the early mornings); and the informality of the Irish way of life. And she missed most of all her beloved Paddy whose request she was now on her way to fulfil.

She looked out of the coach window, busy St-Denis now with its street markets, so different from the *faubourg*, the elegant façade of Ste-Catherine's – Séminaire des Jeunes Filles.

The two young couples in the coach were chattering together, the back of the youngish man looked long-suffering as he bent to hear what the elderly woman – perhaps his

6

mother? – was saying. She caught the courier's eye and he smiled although his face looked anxious. Everyone had their own worries. She leant back . . .

She had been like a worried mother hen when she was away from Paddy. There had always been that look about him. She liked to think that it had nothing to do with Laure. She'd confided her worries to Mhairi.

'You're imagining things. You should be out enjoying yourself with the young folk in the county, balls and such like. He's got his own friends and Paddy Malone is never short of partners, that I know. Sadness! You couldn't find anyone happier than your father, treats everyone alike from the yard lads to Colonel Maguire or the millionaires from America.'

She doesn't have my sensitivity, Nora had thought, dismissing Mhairi with one of those Gallic waves which the school had dispensed with their tuition. She wouldn't confide in her again.

Two

H ome on holiday before her last term, she had seen a change in Paddy. Her darling father was listless, his gaiety was forced. 'Here's my fine little leprechaun home again,' he'd said. The warmth of his arms round her was the same. 'That's the stuff the doctor ordered.' She noticed he stumbled once or twice, and his wan face, his thinness, made her heart ache with anxiety. This time it was Liam who spoke to her. Mhairi was silent.

'Paddy's got my mother worried. He's not eating much and he's complaining of his sight failing. She doesn't want to alarm you.' She had felt faint for a second. 'Why don't you ask him if there's anything wrong? I'm not around so much nowadays. The college keeps me busy.'

'Yes.' But it was really inconsiderate of him not to be around, she thought fretfully and knowing it was unjust. Liam was the only one Paddy allowed to ride his favourites. He had hands like Seumus O'Reilly, his father, he always said.

Liam's grey eyes were on her, reading her like an open book. He'd always been able to do that. Searching. He'd make a good land surveyor. And not a gossip, although he was about the house a fair amount because of his mother. He'd seen Laure in her tantrums. She'd had a soft side for Liam, had made up to him.

'But I'm helping in the yard in the evenings,' he'd said.

8

'And I give his runners a good look-over in the mornings now that he's not up to it . . .' He stopped suddenly, 'Christ! That slipped out. I shouldn't have said it.'

'Don't you keep anything back from me. And watch your mouth, O'Reilly.' Nora withered him with one of her French haughty looks, but fear had taken hold of her like a dog cornering her at a gate.

'Well, he's getting on a bit, isn't he?' Liam had added, looking sheepish.

She spoke to Mhairi later, 'Why didn't you warn me?'

'He didn't want you to be bothered. A sclerotic condition, the doctor says. But you go on in and cheer him up, because as sure as God, it's beyond my power to do it.' She had looked resentful.

He had changed, that was for sure. In her agitation she spoke as roughly as Liam had done; stable talk.

'My God, Paddy, what have you been doing to your eyes? You can't tell one horse from the other from this window! I've been watching you. Have you seen an optician?'

'It's all part and parcel of the same thing. See Flaherty for yourself for I'm fair bamboozled with his long words!' He was jaunty, but there was fear in his eyes.

She saw Dr Flaherty and she refused to go back to Paris. She wrote the letter herself to save Paddy any bother:

Dear Madame de Reignier,
I'm sorry to tell you that my father has multiple sclerosis, so I'm not coming back. Please address any correspondence to me as I'm dealing with his affairs.

Thank you for my education at Ste-Catherine's. I enjoyed it more than I thought, and it pleased my father that I was able to converse in French like my mother.

Merci pour votre gentillesse.

9

She had also written to her mother at her Chelsea flat in London (she felt that if she kept on writing about her father's illness, she might start to believe it):

> Dear Mother,
> You'll be sorry to hear that Paddy has multiple sclerosis.
>
> I don't know if he would want you to know, but I think it is only right. I've left Ste-Catherine's now. You will be glad to hear that you are still remembered there.

When she had first arrived, an elderly mistress had said, 'So *you* are Laure Maguire's daughter!' her eyes sliding sideways.

She settled back in the old house with her father and took over the reins, but was careful not to upset Mhairi. She would have liked to pursue her interest in medieval history at Trinity – indeed she had promised Mademoiselle Vidalle – but her mother had deserted Paddy. She wasn't going to do the same . . .

She swivelled her head on her headrest in the coach, and looked out at gracious forest trees now, behind stone walls running with the coach. They must be getting near the Park.

The disease took four years to kill Paddy: crashing him to the ground; putting him in a wheelchair; taking him out of it; making him feel he had imagined the whole thing; allowing him to entertain, drink, then giving him a side swipe when he was pouring whiskey so that his hand shook and the decanter crashed to the ground. And Laure never came to see him. She wrote to Nora:

> Paddy wouldn't want to see me. In any case I'm going to Phoenix in Arizona with a man I've met, an Amer-

ican called Norman Dexter who comes from there. Kevin cleared out ages ago, thank God. Pure bog Irish that one. I knew. He was only a means to an end.

And there was a note to Paddy which he let her read:

I am sorry that you are ill, but I know you'll be happier with Nora looking after you than me. *Soyez sage! Pas trop tendresse. C'est dangereux!*

I've seen the *notaire* and I'm leaving the house at Lapantelle to her. She's a good girl. She might like it as a bolt-hole?

Bonne chance! Have you got a damp-proof course in that old house yet? Think of me sometimes in sunny Arizona. I'll think of you . . .

P.S. Tell Nora, if she goes to Lapantelle, to light a candle for you at Chartres.

'Maybe it'll be a good thing for you when I . . .' he began but she wouldn't let him say it.

One day, one of his good days, she was sitting beside him at the long windows. Her vision was subtly altered and she looked at her surroundings with a painter's eye. Vlaminck, she thought, taking in the broad sweep of the lawn, the red roofs of the stables, the horizontal lines of the white fencing. She said, as if in reply to his question, 'I'd rather stay with you than go to that French house. Unless you'd rather have mother?'

'I never loved her,' he said. 'You're the only good thing that came out of that.' He put out his hand and laid it on hers. She sat still. Usually she would have put her arms round him, but she was still jealous.

'Why Chartres?' she said, remembering the postscript.

'The house she left you was in a village near it.'

11

'Have you been there?'

'Long ago,' he said, and his brown eyes filled so suddenly that he turned away from her and laughed falsely. 'Give us a hand back to bed, will you? I've been up too long.'

She kissed him on the forehead when she was tucking him in.

The remissions and the pain; the remissions and the falls, the incontinence, was Someone's idea of a joke. It filled up the years. Her twenty-first birthday occurred in the middle of his blindness and there were no candles at home, far less at Chartres. They would have been useless.

She went into the kitchen one night, distraught, when Liam was there. She said to Mhairi, 'He's getting worse. Wouldn't eat a thing. I've phoned the doctor and he'll be round shortly. Maybe you'll take a glass of hot milk to him?'

'I'll do that.' Sometimes her eyes looked boldly at Nora, as if she was irritated by her bossiness, a tug-of-war. 'Away you go with Liam and have a breath of fresh air.' She never thought of her son as anything but a chum for Paddy's daughter. It wasn't that she believed he wasn't good enough for her, just that she never thought of it.

'That's a fine idea,' Liam said. 'And couldn't I do with a breath of fresh air myself, sitting hunched up over them books?'

'Only ten minutes,' Nora said, and when they were walking towards the yard: 'You're losing your golden tan, boyo. The girls won't love you as much.'

'There's only one girl I'm interested in.' He put an arm round her shoulders. 'I'll be a graduate student next year with all those fine letters, and then—'

She interrupted him, 'I've only got one thing in my head at the moment.'

'Sure.' He took his arm away.

They went straight to Starlight's loose box: Paddy's favourite. Nora, watching him, thought, My, he's got the hands of a lover. But then, how the hell should I know?

He turned round, his face lit up with love. 'Did you ever see such a beauty!' he exclaimed.

She met his eyes, distracted, and he turned back again.

'Walters doesn't give her enough attention,' she said. 'That Kevin was good with her, give him his due.' He'd had lover's hands on Laure once. 'Walters worries Paddy on his better days. Says if he were on his feet he'd get rid of him, that the place is losing its reputation. And it the best trainer around from here to Connemara.'

'I could ride Starlight regularly for him in the mornings,' Liam said. 'Early. Before I go to college.'

'I'll tell him.'

It was a fine evening, the air soft and damp, the Wicklow mountains clear; always a sign of rain. A lovely place, this, and what were a few whiffs? Sure, it was just natural.

She turned to Liam, tears in her voice, 'It breaks my heart to see him on his last legs, him so fond of it all.'

He nodded tersely. 'You'll stand up to it.'

She copied the nod. 'I'll get back.'

'Tell him I'd help him up on Starlight's back any time.' She widened her eyes at him.

The doctor warned her that Paddy was sinking fast now. She didn't see Liam around, but Mhairi said he was busy with his finals. 'He goes to the yard every night and does what he can.'

He would, she thought absently.

But Paddy had a strong regard for him. When she asked him if there was anyone he'd like to see, he said, 'Ask Liam to come in, please. He might help me over a bad patch.' She knew he had sacked Walters.

Liam came, neat and clean and pale from his finals and

promised her he wouldn't stay long. He was correct, formal, as if he felt the shadow of death which was hanging over the house, asking everyone to step quietly. When he came out, he said goodnight, formally also, and went away.

Paddy was smiling and at peace when she went in, as if he had no pain. 'Liam's set my mind at ease. He's agreed to take over the running of the place and leave his postgraduate studies till later.'

She was surprised. 'You're putting a load on Liam's shoulders.'

'They're broad enough. And he's offered to help me on to Starlight. My, that will do me good!'

'I think I should mention it to the doctor, Paddy.'

'It's all fixed. There's more medicine than the kind that comes out of a bottle.'

She felt piqued. She told herself that it was because she was anxious, but knew it was more than that.

'You can come too, Nora,' he said with his old jaunty manner.

Her eyes were disapproving as she looked at his useless legs, but that was because of her pique.

She had him showered, padded, dressed and in his chair by six in the morning. He said even his sight was better.

'What I can't see I can fill in,' he said. 'Positive thinking conquers illness. Did you know that? That's the line of the sycamores, isn't it? I can see them waving.'

They had passed the sycamores a few seconds ago.

'We're running over their shadows.'

He was excited. 'Why didn't we think of this before? You and I will be going for runs in the old Rolls next, visiting friends, going to balls, race meetings. And there's those quiet nights at the fire . . . Oh, there's a fine life ahead for us, Nora.'

Liam was there before them. He had Starlight ready, and

had fixed a cradle on her back that he had used when he was teaching the disabled from the nearby home.

'Where's the crane, Liam?' Paddy said, laughing, man to man.

'There's no need for that, no need for that at all.' He lifted him out of the wheelchair and set him on the horse's back, as light as a feather. 'As good as an armchair, are you thinking?'

'Better. It's moving.' His hands were so curled up in balls and useless that Liam tied the reins to his wrists.

'Remember, we don't want you thinking you're winning the St-Leger. Just a nice gentle trot.' He had two other horses saddled, and he and Nora mounted and took their places on either side of him.

'Here comes the cavalcade!' Nora said. The sharp air was in her nostrils. My, it was a fine thing to do, this. She had forgotten how good it was.

'*Le Défilé de Presentation des Pouliches*!' Paddy shouted, and when she looked at him his head was up and he was looking straight ahead with his fine profile.

She caught Liam's questioning glance and shook her head, implying, he's fine.

They turned when they had been twice round the paddock and this time she noticed Paddy's head had sunk forward. But he was secure in his cradle. It was just that his weak back had given in.

'That's enough of a good thing, Paddy,' Liam said. 'We'll make for home now.' He met Nora's look, held it, and nodded. His face was a mask of sadness.

She froze, felt nothing. Nothing. Nothing! She wanted to feel, desperately, but was too cold to feel.

Once Liam had lifted Paddy's body down from the cradle and strapped it in his wheelchair, she allowed him to push it back to the house. Her legs were useless. His weren't. And he wasn't weeping. He put an arm round her waist to help her along. The tears were running down her face, like Irish rain, blinding her.

That winter of 1989, when she was clearing out his papers, she found an envelope in his desk, fat and bulky. On the front he had written, 'Chantilly, 1962.' She sat at the long window all afternoon reading its contents. The broad sweep of lawn had a light sprinkling of snow on it. Mist was swirling round the red roofs of the stables. It looked sad, as if in memory of Paddy. On one page the words had sprung out at her: *Prix de Diane Hermès, Défilé de Presentation des Pouliches*. Parade of Three-year-old Fillies didn't sound nearly as grand. But Paddy had remembered the French words.

When she closed the envelope she saw the deformed scrawl on the back of it. 'Go in June, Nora, will you? For your Paddy.'

She raised her head and thought she saw his jaunty figure coming over the lawn towards her, smiling, trim, the trilby over his eyes, his striped tie, checked jacket, tan breeches, polished boots, stock in his hand. He seemed to emerge from the mist, but when she half-rose, he had disappeared.

Three

The sun shone and it seemed the whole world was *en fête* as they drove through the gates. The driver chose a pleasant spot in the park, and the courier invited them all to dismount and place their bets while he prepared their *repas*. He was young, smiling, but his smile was still anxious. Everyone had their own problems.

The two young couples broke the ice because they were so happy and were squeezing every ounce of happiness out of the day as if it were a juicy orange. They chattered as the seven of them walked towards the booking booths. The elderly lady became graciously informative, gathering them around her. The youngish man stood slightly apart.

'Perhaps I can explain the system to you, if you haven't been here before. There aren't any bookmakers in French racecourses. You just go to the appropriate window when you've chosen your horse. Give the number, or numbers. You've got your racecards.'

'How do you know which window?' one of the young men asked.

'It's according to the amount of francs you wish to put on.'

Nora could see the elderly lady at the Townswomen's Guild in, say, Cheltenham? She put on a listening face.

'*Gagnant* is to win. Each way, *gagnant et placé*. Do you understand?'

'Oh, dear!' one of the pretty young girls wailed, the

fair one. She looked appealingly at the young man beside her.

'But in races 2 and 4 only,' Nora said, looking innocent, 'that is, a straight forecast, you pick two horses to come first and second in the correct order. That's called *jumelé*. In all the other races it doesn't matter in what order.' She saw the steely look of the gracious elderly woman.

'Where do you collect your winnings?' One of the young men addressed himself to Nora.

'At any window which deals with the amount of your stake.'

'Well, now that our friend has explained the system,' the elderly woman said, studiously gracious, 'I think you should place your bets now. It gets very busy especially at the 10 franc and 50 franc windows.'

'Be sure and keep your betting slips,' Nora called after the party as they set off.

The youngish man turned to her, 'Aren't you coming?'

She smiled and shook her head.

You're a tease, Nora. Paddy's voice echoed in her head as she turned away. Well, yes . . .

After the triumphal procession and the hats, no better than Phoenix Park or Leopardstown, she registered, she watched what she had come for, the parade of the three-year-old fillies, more elegant than the hatted ladies, *Défilé de Pre-sentation des Pouliches*. I'm here, Paddy, as you wished, twenty-seven years later. She stood with her eyes closed, as if at a wake. After a long time, she walked back to where the coach was parked and where the young Frenchman had spread out rugs on the grass, inviting them all to sit in the sun. Apparently satisfied with the Sisley-esque arrangement, he distributed the promised hampers.

'*Servez-vous!*' he said gaily, and helped by the three men he began opening champagne bottles. With the release of corks, and pouring of the wine, the party of disparate people became a small friendly group.

'I'm Maddy, and this is Emma,' one of the young girls said, the dark one, 'and these two heart-throbs with the bottles are Graham and Derek – he's the tall skinny one. The four of us are in Paris for a dirty weekend.'

'I'm Nora,' Nora said. 'I'm here because I promised my father who died six months ago.' And I miss him like Bejasus. Which she didn't say.

'Grace Trant –' the elderly woman bowed graciously – 'and this is my son, Richard. He's located in Paris for his firm. I'm visiting him for the weekend.'

'I could think of worse places to be located,' Richard Trant said with a slanting smile at Nora.

She didn't like being singled out, and returned an equally slanting smile. I'm sure his mother comes from Cheltenham, she thought. It had been Paddy's favourite English event and he'd had a winner once or twice at the festival there.

In spite of the general bonhomie, Nora also noticed that, like her, no one was giving too much away. It was to be a fun day, a day apart from other days, a little plateau where everyone was a stranger but able to communicate with everyone else because they had one thing in common: a day at the races.

They all began to open their hampers with suitably excited squeals from Maddy and Emma. They chatted and laughed and Grace Trant put on her large-brimmed hat to look the part, she said. Maddy and Emma took off their high-heeled shoes, wiggled their toes and said, 'Utter bliss.' They looked delectable in their bell-shaped short skirts, and Nora could quite understand their appeal for Graham and Derek who looked besotted.

It was a beautiful day, an *Après-midi d'un Faune* day, a daydream of a day. The nearby chateau swam in a heat haze;

19

there was the distant sound of voices; an occasional roar as a horse fell, or reached the tape, or jostled, or unseated its rider and bolted. It was like a well worn tape to Nora. She saw Paddy, glasses round his neck, hat tipped forward, smartly suited, striped tie, with his thin, brown face which had drained parchment white when he had died, sitting on Starlight.

After lunch and much talking, she lay back, unpaired, but glad, and looked at the blue French sky and thought of him.

'When I go you'll have no-one,' he'd said one night when they'd been sitting at the log fire in the hall. He'd bent forward and stroked her cheek. She had turned her head so that she kissed his hand. She met his eyes, warm from the fire . . . or something else? She heard her mother's words, '*Pas trop de tendresse. C'est dangereux.*' A warning voice. Think of Liam instead, she told herself, when he'd been saying goodbye before this trip to France.

'I'll be thinking of you,' he'd said.

'Yes, well,' she'd said, 'but I'm thinking of a French count or someone important in the Diplomatic Corps.' She knew him too well . . .

'Your mother made the mistake of educating you in Paris,' he'd said. His eyes had looked sad behind the banter.

The French sun was hot as she lay there, but it was the soft damp wind of Ireland which was on her face. She was outside the tack room at the back of the house watching Liam as he groomed Mavourneen, his own mare. He had broad shoulders, a slim waist, hips like a Flamenco dancer, head well set. Yes, better to think of Liam . . .

'Having a bit of a kip?' It was Grace Trant's son looking down at her.

'Caught in the act.' She sat up, slowly. 'Where is everybody?'

'The courier's gone to look at pictures in the chateau (has

20

no time for racing), my mother's off eagle-eyed with the other four to collect their winnings. She loves race-going. Comes from Cheltenham.' Right first time.

'Aren't you going back?'

'Oh, yes. I wondered if you were in need of an escort?'

'An escort?' She smiled, questioningly.

'You know. At the booths.'

'*Guichets*. But I didn't bet.'

'I'd forgotten. *Guichets*? That's it. I heard you chattering away in French with the courier like nobody's business.'

'His wife's about to have a baby. He's anxious.'

'Poor chap. He'll be consoling himself by looking at art.'

Les Très Riches Heures, she thought. She had gone to see them with the school. 'No, he's delirious with joy, actually.'

She was glad to be talking about the courier. She had listened sympathetically to all his worries when they were eating: his little wife might go into labour while he was at work; how would they contact him, how would they ever get a bassinet up the stairs to their attic apartment, the cost of numerous little jackets and diapers . . . you can't imagine . . .

'Maybe you'd like to have a go at the *guichets* now?' Grace Trant's son had a charming smile, but an eye that seemed to have looked at a lot of women. He was slimmer than Liam in the shoulders with thin hands like his face, and a tautness, a kind of *nervosité* about him. She wondered if he were married. One side of his mouth turned down slightly, which she had seen sometimes in married men. She took it as a sign of disappointment.

'No, thanks,' she said. 'I just came for the *Défilé*.'

He was puzzled but hid it. 'Oh, well, in that case. If you don't mind being left alone . . .'

'No, not at all.' She squinted up at him because of the sunlight. 'And the *ambiance*.' She smiled. Liam had told her once she had a smile to break anyone's heart, and she used it.

21

Not a hint of Paddy's leprechaun one. He was attractive, this Richard, but she was here because of Paddy, and to think. 'Good luck!' she said.

She lay down when he'd gone and tried to slip back to remembering the good times, but there was a layer of sadness now. She couldn't conjure up that old house with its wide windows and its stone steps leading up to the grand door, the worn rugs in the firelit hall, the permanent faint smell of damp that the bowls of flowers Liam's mother placed everywhere tried to disguise, and the dogs.

Yes, she said to herself (she often started sentences with 'yes' like Molly Bloom), I'm an heiress sure enough with that old house left to me by Paddy and the other one that my mother has left me at Lapantelle which I've never seen. 'In the middle of the Beauce,' Paddy had said. 'Sure and to God, it's like the golden sea and aren't I the poet?' He'd put an arm round her waist and squeezed it.

She remembered going with Ste-Catherine's on a visit to the cathedral at Chartres. She wouldn't mind seeing those rose windows again, especially the north one, jewel-like. That blue, *bleu de Chartres*, it was called. And the corbels. She had nudged her best friend, Antoinette, and been withered by a glance from Madame Vidalle. She had been ashamed, remembering she had told the mistress that she would like to study medieval history.

She could do anything now. 'You being an heiress makes me wonder if I should touch my forelock to you,' Liam had said. At times he was a hell of a fellow, Liam, all the girls were daft about him. Yes, but she knew him too well . . . Besides she had to do a lot of thinking first, sort herself out, look into herself and her grief.

There was that time, during one of Paddy's remissions (a long one) when they'd had a cosy night at the hall fire with the dogs and they'd had a whiskey or two as he'd told her about the great wins he'd had with Shagreen: 'The best horse I ever trained. The heart of a warrior. Seumus won five times on him that season, a champion.' And she'd got up, yawning, and said, 'Well, it's me for the wooden hill,' and bent down as usual to kiss his forehead. She had laughed, saying, 'Whiskey breath!'

Afterwards, she had remembered her mother's words, '*Pas trop de tendresse. C'est dangereux.*'

Mhairi had said the following morning when she'd gone into the kitchen, 'My God, you look like a ghost.'

She'd looked at Mhairi and thought, well, you don't. She had a bloom about her. She was a fine-looking woman, but this was something extra.

She'd been straight with Liam. 'I'm restless since Paddy died. There's this space in my life that he filled. I have this emptiness. I still weep. I've to go to the races at Chantilly – he asked me – then see my French house and then—'

'There's the French count or the diplomat?'

She smiled at him. 'You know me. I'm a joker.'

Now, she lay on the rug in the grounds of that big chateau with its fine statues and waterfalls, and thought only of the old house, and Paddy. This second stage of grieving was worse than the first. It hurts, she said to Paddy, in her mind, here – as she put her hand on her heart – so badly. I'm trying to get myself straight, but it's still only you and I can't stand anyone else intruding on your private space . . .

Those nights after he died when she couldn't sleep, she'd sat at the side window which looked out over the fields and had seen his jaunty figure striding out of the morning mist towards the back door, and she'd rushed down to open it, time and time again, smiling the leprechaun smile . . . and he wasn't there. And one night she had howled, like a creature in the darkness, and she said to Liam's mother in the morning, 'Did you hear that owl last night, Mhairi? Howling?' And she'd said, 'Oh, was that what it was, screeching like a banshee? I nearly jumped out of my skin.'

But later, she remembered that there were never any owls around the house. Liam had told her that and one night when she was helping in the yard, he had led her into the barn and said, 'Funny they never come near the house. Just the barn.' At the time she'd thought it was a dodge, just like the others, thinking up tricks to get her alone.

But he hadn't laid a finger on her. 'Shh!' he had said, taking her by the hand to sit on a bale of hay. And she'd seen it.

'A young male,' he'd said. Its round black eyes set closely on either side of the curved beak had held hers steadily, without blinking. It hadn't moved, nor had she. Its feathers were creamy white. She'd had to tear her eyes away as if it had mesmerized her.

'Frightening,' she'd said.

'But beautiful. A barn owl.'

'But . . .' No, she wouldn't say it.

The others came back. Grace Trant looked pleased with herself, her large-brimmed hat quite jaunty now and escorted by her son who wasn't at all jaunty. He had either lost money or was fed up being a dutiful son. Maddy and Emma were ecstatic at their wins and Graham and Derek were quieter than earlier. 'It's better with bookies!' she heard Derek say, the long skinny one.

I wouldn't have them, girls, she thought, they're bad losers. Maybe there'll be no *bateau mouche* dinner now.

The young Frenchman came back seemingly spiritually fortified by dousing himself in art and said, 'There are still three bottles of champagne.' Only a Frenchman could pronounce it like 'shawmpaagne,' caressingly, deep-vowelled. 'Please share it amongst you while I pack the hampers and rugs into the coach and warn the driver. I think we should get back before the traffic really hots up.'

Nora was sure he'd had a telepathic message from his little wife that she was going into labour.

They were very jolly with their last drinks. The girls, good sorts, Maddy and Emma, offered to pay for the dinners on the *bateau mouche*. Grace Trant said she had done 'rather well' with her *jumelé* and, the champagne loosening her tongue, confided that her son was an architect, but felt Paris rather lonely at times. 'Home ties, you know.' Nora didn't know whether that meant he was married.

He smiled rather cagily and said to everyone that they should really try to see the Pompidou Centre, 'A joke, really, it reminds me of someone caught in their underwear.' He looked around for a laugh and Nora sent one side of her mouth upwards.

Then Derek, awed seemingly, asked his opinion about the Barbican. 'Well, if you like concrete barns . . .' Nora tried the other side of her mouth.

They filed into the coach at the courier's request and Grace said to the son, a little tipsily, 'You sit with Nora, Richard. I want to have a snooze on the way back.'

Nora couldn't object. In a way, she was glad not to sit beside the courier as her knowledge of the different stages of labour were minimal – she had helped Daisy, her spaniel, once or twice, and once a mare with twins; one was born dead and the stable lad had wheeled it away in a barrow like a sack of potatoes.

Richard had forgiven her for her coldness – actually the champagne had mellowed her as well – and seemed determined to be charming, which he was. 'Are you staying in Paris?' he asked.

'No,' she said, 'I'm going on to a small village near Chartres.' She didn't give its name, nor any reason why she was going there, but she felt well-disposed towards him and asked intelligent (she hoped) questions about his work while not saying anything about her own. As a matter of fact, she was ashamed that she didn't have any work. A spoiled brat, she said to herself. Yes. Who had been obsessed by her father . . . still was. Well, yes . . .

'I intend to visit as many cathedrals as possible while I'm in Paris,' he said. 'Always wanted to. Chartres is a must.'

'The rose windows?'

'No, it's the flying buttresses, actually. Perhaps we could meet in Chartres sometime?'

'Perhaps.' Her voice trailed away. Paddy was there again, at Leopardstown, leading in Shagreen, 'The big black bastard' he called the stallion, laughing all over his face. 'He's done it again! Nora, come into the picture too!' Putting his arm round her, pulling her close.

'Would you like to fix a time and place?' Richard Trant was there again, smiling his charming but practised smile.

'Shall we leave it that we may bump into each other?' She saw the smile fade. I don't want to be cruel, she thought, it's just that Paddy gets in the way. My mind is full of him. It's boring for other people . . . but it hurts, oh, it hurts. It's the void. He took up such a big place in my heart. Had it been too big a place, no room for anyone else, for Liam?

But you could fill it if you wanted, she thought as they bowled along. There's any amount of youngish attractive men like this one . . . not too many French counts, or diplomats. She looked out of the window of the coach and saw all the open cars, people waving and shouting and she waved back, touched by their pleasure. Liam could fill her father's place. 'You're . . . easy with Liam, always have been . . .' Paddy used to say.

When they were dropped off opposite the Tuileries, they all said goodbye, laughingly. Such a fun day. The girls were still carrying their shoes and in their bell skirts they looked like flowers. Graham and Derek were beaming, possibly because they had been assured about the *bateau mouche* dinners.

Grace Trant was gracious and her son pleasant, but his eyes were watchful of Nora as if she might lash out with her hooves, or their equivalent. 'I'll look out for you in Chartres,' she said gaily, to flummox him.

When they looked round for the young courier to thank him (Derek had passed round a paper bag for the *pour-boire*), he had gone. Very un-French. The imminent arrival of his first child had been more important.

'If you're willing to trust me,' Nora said, 'I have to come back here tomorrow and I could hand in the money. I want to hire a car.' The two couples murmured their consent and Richard Trant smiled absently. He looked as if he wanted to dump his mother more than anything else.

Nora said goodbye and crossed the road to the gardens. She would walk about a little until she felt like going back to her hotel. She went through the ornate gilded gates and turning back she could see Richard Trant standing looking after her, his hand through his mother's arm. Ships that pass, she thought, walking briskly along the asphalt path. When she felt she was safely out of sight, she sat down on a bench enjoying the warm dryness of the French sun.

Well, I've been to Chantilly, Paddy, and it was just the same. Twenty-seven years since you met mother, Laure Maguire, there. I'm the result, twenty-three, a year younger than you were. What does it signify? It can't be her you want to remember since you said you never wanted to marry her in the first place. Was it the other girl? You've left me with a puzzle.

The beneficent sun soothed her. I'm going to train my mind to look outwards, she promised herself, absorb my surroundings, stay in my French house and have French dreams instead of Irish ones. She got up purposefully. Now, I'm going to go back to my hotel, have dinner and some wine and then an early night.

Some wine ended up being half a bottle of Vouvray and a tot of brandy from the courtesy cabinet and she fell into bed feeling pleasantly drowsy; when she closed her eyes the soft damp air stroked her cheeks and she knew she was back at Marchmount.

But not Paddy again, please God. I've been to Chantilly . . . An owl shriek filled her ears for a second, terrifying her, filling her with dread, then the brandy and the wine won. She slept dreamlessly.

In the morning she felt fine and rested and thought of Liam while she dressed. He would be in charge now and running the place as efficiently as Paddy would have liked it. Or herself, since it belonged to her now.

Why had Liam decided to go to college to study earth sciences as he called it, when he was so nicely settled at Marchmount? Had it been her derogatory remarks about stable smells that had irritated him? But that had been when she was seventeen and stupid and imbued with the French way and all those glorious perfumes she read about in Parisian magazines and smelled on the girls at Ste-Catherine's – and her mother's remark. Anyhow, you could say anything to Liam – one always did in the old days.

Now, he had agreed to run Marchmount – had it been for her? she wondered. Would his mother have told him he could move in? She might, but Liam wouldn't do that. There was a sensitivity in him, not apparent in his mother, like the highly-bred horses he looked after, a delicacy of feeling. Mhairi instead was earthy, fleshy, bosomy.

But she'd been different since Paddy had died, going about

her work without her usual bustle, but that wasn't surprising. She had been grateful to Paddy for giving her a job. She wouldn't be so sure about his daughter.

Nora was feeling so good that she seemed to float on the light summer air down the Rue St Honoré to the tourist office where she handed over the *pour-boire*. 'The courier isn't here?' she asked the young man behind the counter, an equally dapper young man.

'Alas, no.' He looked at Nora as if assessing whether he could be more explicit.

'Has his wife had her baby?' she asked.

He smiled broadly, nodding. 'You knew? Armand was very anxious yesterday. Yes, a little boy. He won't be in for a week or so. The management is very considerate in such cases.'

'Good. Perhaps the *pour-boire* will buy the baby a pair of *petits chaussons*.' The French bootees she had seen in shop windows were pretty enough to drool over.

'You're very kind. I'll see Armand gets this.'

'I'm going to Lapantelle, a village near Chartres. Do you know of it?'

'I'm afraid not.'

'I'd like to hire a car if possible and drive there today.'

'Certainly. If I may make a suggestion, mademoiselle, there is an hourly train to Chartres from Gare Montparnasse which would avoid you having to drive on the *périphérique* out of Paris, if you're not accustomed to it.'

'That might be better. I shall have to see the house agent in Chartres in any case before I go to the village.'

'I could arrange for the car to be left at Chartres station and you could pick up the keys at their *guichet*.'

The idea appealed to her. She rarely drove the Rolls to Dublin nowadays because of the difficulty in parking and she really didn't want to get involved in the Paris *périphérique*.

'That's excellent. I expect I shall have to do some shopping before I go to Lapantelle in any case.'

The preliminaries were settled amicably. She chose a Peugeot recommended by the young man, passed over her documents and the payment necessary, and emerged from the office pleased with her arrangements.

It was good to be back in Paris again and she had a tour round the Galeries Lafayette for old time's sake. Madame de Reignier had allowed the girls to shop there, chaperoned, of course, and combined with a tour of the Opera House before for *la culture Française*. She had a cursory look at Notre Dame, short because she intended to spend time in the cathedral at Chartres, bought some postcards and sat at a café table in the sun writing them.

The Seine was as serene as ever; the *bateaux mouches* went fussily about their business. She felt at home; she had lived here so there was no need to set out on a tourist trail. She wrote a card to Liam:

> Arrived safely in Paris and have fixed up a car. I'm going to the house this afternoon. Lovely to be here. Hope all goes well with you at Marchmount. Nora.

He could let his mother read it if she wished.

She had temporarily abandoned the house; she didn't want to be tied to it any more than was necessary. This was free time, time to reflect. It seemed to be the first time in her life when she was really independent. No one to lean on, to advise her, to love her . . . She felt her heart give a lurch, her spirits plunge.

She got up and walked down the steps to the river bank, close to tears. When would she have a mind free of Paddy, snippets of Paddy, his beguiling smile, his way with words that made her laugh, his beryl-brown eyes, with that twinkle, his uniqueness?

She would walk back to her hotel, pack, then ring for a taxi to take her to Gare Montparnasse. After she was installed in her house at Lapantelle, she could have day trips to Paris and go to the Louvre – you always meant to go to the Louvre but never did – see a play, buy some clothes. Chartres would be her market town and she'd make a habit of driving there and back so that she could see the twin spires of the cathedral rising up from the Beauce, 'like a golden sea'. *And aren't I the poet?*

Four

Nora's first impression, as she drove towards the Place Chatelet, where she had been directed by the clerk at the station who had handed over the keys for the Peugeot, was that Chartres was a small city rather than a town. The post office, as she passed it, looked like a medieval castle.

I suppose it has a lot to live up to, she thought, seeing the two spires of the cathedral sailing above it.

When she announced herself in the estate office, she was shown into a room where a pretty young woman shook hands with her and asked her to sit down.

'I'm Mademoiselle Bettine Coton.' She smiled. 'I'm very pleased to meet the new owner of Le Manoir Lapantelle. I understand it has been left to you by your mother, Madame Dexter, it says?' She had a file open in front of her.

'Yes, that's right. She remarried recently.'

'Ah, that explains it.' Nora recognized the curiosity of the average Frenchwoman. 'Allow me to congratulate you, Mademoiselle Malone. It's a very nice small property – I've seen it – with very large gates!' She smiled again.

'Has it? I wonder why?'

'I'm comparatively new here so I may be wrong, but I wondered if it had tumbled down, or been set on fire. . .' Her smile was fetching. She was very pretty.

'And you mean that the present house was built in its

place?' Her mother hadn't said, but then they hadn't been in close communication for years.

'Something like that. Anyhow, the present one is in good condition.'

'Is it fully furnished?'

'Oh, yes. And we do look after our properties. One of us drives out every week to see that all is well, and there's a caretaker with keys in the row of cottages round the corner from it.' She looked down at the file lying on her desk. 'Three bedrooms, sitting room and the usual kitchen etc. And there's a guest cottage.' She looked up. 'Strangely enough, your mother left it to a friend who lives in America –' she looked down quickly and up again – 'a Mrs Roberta Clancy.'

'Oh!' She remembered Mhairi saying her husband had talked about another girl with Laure at Chantilly that year.

Mademoiselle Coton had seen her hesitation. 'It's quite a distance from your house. It shouldn't worry you.'

'Is she there just now?'

'No, I'm sure she isn't. We would know.' She changed the subject as she continued, 'Do you plan to go there today, mademoiselle?'

'Yes, if it's ready for occupancy.' Nothing was straightforward, she thought. The girl was acute.

'The beds are made up. I wonder . . . would you like someone to go with you? Your first visit . . . It could be arranged.' Her eyes were rounded, hopeful.

'No, thanks.' She wanted to think about things. 'Perhaps you'd be kind enough to telephone the caretaker and tell her I'm on my way. Is it far?'

'Fifteen minutes. You have a car?' She was lifting the telephone, her eyes on Nora, who nodded.

'Ah, Madame Leroux! *Je m'excuse, mais . . .*'

Nora listened to the girl's quick French chatter, the familiar politenesses, with some affection.

'Madame Leroux awaits you.' She had hung up.

'Thank you. You've been very kind.'

'You're sure you don't want . . . no, but you said . . .' persisted the girl.

Do I look too pathetic or young? Nora thought. How *do* I look to other people? I've been incarcerated at Marchmount for four years, more or less, by my own choice. Paddy filled my life. Has it made me different? This girl, probably my own age, will meet friends after work, she'll have a drink with them at a café, chatter, laugh . . . I'd be more at home with horses . . . Give it up! She chided herself.

She put the documents and the spare set of keys in her handbag. 'Is it a pretty village?' she asked.

'Pretty? Well, I wouldn't call it that. It's a walled village, at least, there are high walls round most of the properties, and it gives it rather a . . . forbidding aspect? A secret village, but that, of course, is what one wants with *une maison secondaire, n'est ce pas*? I seem to remember there's a water tower nearby . . . yes . . . and *le place* is sanded, and not even a café around where one could sit in the sun with friends. But, then, I like Chartres. So much life. So modern and up-to-date.'

Had she noticed the cathedral? Nora wondered, then said aloud, 'Yes, it's certainly that.' And, on an impulse, thinking she might need a friend, 'When I come to do some shopping, possibly on market days, perhaps you could slip out and we could have a coffee together?'

'Su–per!' The girl smiled enthusiastically. 'Any time, Mademoiselle Malone, any time!' She put her hand to her chin, glancing at Nora. 'Perhaps I've been a little . . . disparaging about Lapantelle. You will probably find it a very jolly village; there are other people, naturally, and they will play bridge: that is what they do in the afternoons, the Parisians, I believe, and give private dinners . . . since there is no café . . .'

Nora laughed. 'I don't play bridge. And I'm here for a

rest.' And to sort myself out, maybe become like this pretty Bettine . . . but not too much.

Mademoiselle Coton had a good eye, Nora decided later when she drove into the empty square. Two dogs circling each other were the only signs of life. Walls – certainly high – hid the houses presumably, but gave Lapantelle the appearance of being deserted. And there, rearing above her was the water tower Bettine had spoken about.

Madame Leroux had surrendered the keys but hadn't been disposed to gossip, or even look particularly pleasant. Perhaps Nora had come at a bad time. There had been a rich smell of onions in the background, probably her husband's supper. Her door had opened off the street and there was no attempt to prettify the place with hanging baskets or tubs of flowers, which was unusual. Nor any sound of children's voices.

And, now, here were the gates – massive gates – worthy of a chateau. Through them she could see a large rough lawn and in the distance a smallish house, but there was no drive. The guest cottage was invisible from where she stood.

She parked the car outside the gates, got out and, selecting a key which was larger than the rest, inserted it in the lock. One gate swung slowly open. She went inside as if into a prison.

Five

S he realized the following morning, she had been tired before and her impression of the village had been coloured by that tiredness.

Her first two days in the house passed without her speaking to anyone at all, and consequently Paddy was always in her mind. Here, she hadn't even the comfort of a well known background like Marchmount, but after the first day when she had felt disorientated and unhappy, her natural resilience reasserted itself, and she began to take an interest in her surroundings.

First of all, she decided, she would make a tour of the house, which wouldn't compare with a tour of Marchmount. There were no corridors, no hidden corners, the design was simple, box-like. The large kitchen–dining room which gave on to the front, had a pleasant old-fashioned appeal with its pine furniture and blue-and-white checked cushions and curtains. The smaller sitting room on the other side of the hall was not so welcoming; darker, since it had a single window, possibly intended for winter evenings because there was a fine old stone fireplace, rather too large for the size of the room.

At the back of the house, there were two large bedrooms which looked over the fields; fields upon fields, fields upon more fields, merging into the golden Beauce panorama and into the horizon. Upstairs was an attic bedroom with the same view but even more far-reaching. A light house, she thought, except for the small sitting room.

Outside, there was no attempt at a patio, only the large rough lawn, on which there sat a substantial table of oak with six equally sturdy chairs. The whole place gave the impression of a holiday house, a place for sleeping and eating, indoors or out, with nothing which could spoil.

The garden could be improved: some beds cut out of the lawn, paths laid, a few bushes planted, a little landscaping to take away the bareness of the view from the windows and possibly attempt to conceal the sight of the guest cottage.

She walked the length of the lawn to the huge gates, looked through and saw the Peugeot still there, turned to her right and went over to have a closer look at the guest cottage tucked in at the side: a white-painted pavilion-type building with a veranda approached by a flight of wooden steps. She felt momentarily sorry that it didn't belong to her as well. She went back to the gates again, peered through and saw nothing but a deserted road.

I'm behaving like an animal which has been in captivity too long, she thought. I can go out at any time, but it would have been reassuring to have seen a few people strolling about. Such peace is what the Parisians pay money for, she told herself, and there may be some inhabitants here already, glad of their high walls. Just wait till the August holiday . . .

At least there was Madame Leroux, she thought, and very likely a Monsieur Leroux who cut the grass regularly, or it would have resembled a hayfield. She could soon find out.

Her spirits were rising. She had a project in view which would at least partially fill her mind: new furnishings to be bought in Chartres, and a visit to the market there would supply her with the eucalyptus and bay trees, the rhododendrons, azaleas and similar greenery for planting, and plenty of annuals and perennials which would go into the beds to be cut out of the lawn. Perhaps a patio could be laid and furnished with bright garden chairs and an umbrella.

And a vegetable garden was an essential. She almost preferred that to a flower garden. Old Aidan at Marchmount had passed on his lore. He was, as Paddy put it, 'A dab hand with the tatties,' and she had always found it satisfying to see the long rows of the feathery foliage of carrots, the fresh green of lettuces, the topknots of potatoes and turnips.

She began to open one of the gates every day and go for long walks round the village and beyond, but except for an occasional farmer on a tractor or someone working in the fields, she saw no one, nor did she come across any school.

A French village was different from an Irish one, she told herself. There was nothing cosily familiar about it, as at Marchmount with its gentle hilliness and boskiness, the small farms around with their proliferation of hens, cows and pigs, people working about and always ready to stop and have a crack with you. Here, in the Beauce, because of the immensity of the fields, the desolation seemed to echo the seeming emptiness of Lapantelle.

She called on Madame Leroux at what seemed a more convenient time than before, and found her willing to talk, but not with the natural garrulousness of her own folk. Yes, her husband tended the lawn at Le Manoir. Yes, he wouldn't mind having extra work to do if he got paid for it. He had a fine vegetable garden at the back of the house and would be willing to do more.

'It's a very quiet village,' Nora said.

The woman nodded and shrugged as she replied, 'August will be busier. The children are still at school in Paris, and the mamas like to be there for the season.'

'Does their presence make a lot of difference to the village?' Nora asked.

'Not a great deal. They tend to entertain in their own

38

homes – most of them have pools – or drive to Chartres in the evening to Le Boeuf Coronné or the other one. And, of course, there is bridge. The roads become busier then, with the ladies driving here and there.'

I, too, could have a pool, Nora had registered. She told herself she was getting an insight into French holiday culture, and the difference between the French and the Irish villager. She had only known Paris. But she was adaptable. While in Rome . . . She would draw out a plan.

But she had to accept it. Lapantelle was never going to be a St-Tropez, and unless she grew to love it, which wasn't impossible, Le Manoir was never going to be anything but a holiday home. Marchmount was still where she wanted to be, where Paddy was, or had been, and where she felt at home. How long, she wondered, would it take to be able to live there and not be haunted by his presence?

Would she sell up eventually and buy a seaside home on the Bay in Dublin which was something Paddy always said he would do when he got tired of the upkeep at Marchmount – a threat made every month when he was paying bills and then promptly forgotten. And there was Liam, now in her employ. She saw vividly for a second his tanned, strong face, the look in his eyes when they rested on her, contained, steady, patient.

A wave of homesickness swept over her. What was she doing here in this strange country, this strange house? She should have stayed in Paris after her visit to the racecourse, then gone back home again. All she was doing was running away from memories. Paddy, her dear Paddy, whom she had loved so much, Marchmount, Liam . . .

She went to bed that night, her optimism gone, and whether it was because of all her walking and planning, to her surprise and relief she slept dreamlessly.

The following morning she was cheerful, back to plan-

ning. First, she thought, I must look around the shops –
they should be good in Chartres – and see what they had in
them to give Le Manoir a bit of her own identity. And food,
she thought. What's the use of living in France and not
taking advantage of the food? Remember those luscious
pears we used to get at Ste-Catherine's? And being repri-
manded for having the juice dripping down our chins?
August, of course, but what about those delicacies *tartes
des framboises*?

Bettine, she thought, would give her expert advice on
where to shop. She lifted the telephone, dialled the number
she found in her diary and soon heard the girl's voice rippling
like running water over the wire.

'Allo, allo! Mademoiselle Coton here.'

'Do you remember me? It's Nora Malone.'

'*Ah, mademoiselle*! *Quel plaisir*!' She gave an excited little
squeal. 'How are you getting on in the great metropolis?
Comprenez-vous?' A little gale of laughter.

'*Mais oui*! *Très bien, merci*. I've settled down now, and
have made friends with Madame Leroux.'

'*Ah bon*! And next month all Paris will be there – even if
they only rush past in cars!' Her laugh tinkled.

'*D'accord*! Would you be able to slip out and meet me,
mademoiselle? I'm coming in to shop.'

'*Avec plaisir*. I could meet you for morning coffee at, say,
l'hôtel de France? They have a *jolie terrasse* there.'

'That sounds fine.' She was quite willing to be led about by
Bettine. 'Shall we say eleven o'clock there?'

The drive into Chartres was more than pleasant, it was an
experience: the huge golden expanse of wheatfields in front
of her; in the foreground the gold separating into a haze of
colours; the blue of cornflowers or wild salvias, the scarlet
of poppies; and on the horizon the twin spires of the
cathedral.

The sight moved her deeply. The purity and nobility of the scene in front of her seemed to lift her to a different plane of thought. She must begin to look forward, realize how lucky she was, a young woman of property. With Paddy around, or because of him, she had avoided friends of her own age, and they in turn had avoided her. She had been like a statue that time when Liam had put his arms around her. Girls of twenty-three nowadays were experienced, had had sexual encounters, whereas she had remained an adolescent, obsessed by her father. Wasn't it time to grow up, to gain some of that experience?

The spires were growing taller as she drew near Chartres, and with her eyes on them from time to time, she drove steadily, feeling as if a weight had been lifted from her.

Bettine, when Nora met her in the hotel, was as bubbly as ever, smart in a short black sleeveless dress and high-heeled court shoes. She greeted Nora effusively, exchanged small talk while they drank coffee, and proved to be as helpful as she was bubbly.

She had a friend who kept the most exclusive shop in Chartres. She could take Nora to meet her tomorrow, Saturday. Regrettably, she would have to get back to the office now, Friday being a busy day.

'She would give you the best advice and show you the choicest fabrics outside Paris. And her lampshades are to dream about!' Bettine enthused. And later on, if Nora wished it, they could both come to Lapantelle and help her with her improvements. Denise's taste, Bettine assured her, was *ravissant*. She went twinkling off on her high heels after effusive kisses and hand wavings.

Nora blew out her breath and thought, Gosh! I'm too reserved! That's from being segregated at Ste-Catherine's, and being always with Paddy in the holidays.

She was no longer on the high and rarefied plane she'd

been on when driving into Chartres, but it was there in her mind. Fixed. It was time to change.

She remembered Bettine's parting remark: 'The three of us will have all afternoon to choose what you want, but I must leave you not a minute after five o'clock. My boyfriend . . . he becomes too possessive!' She had closed her eyes, put a hand to her heart and sighed with delight. Hadn't Liam once said, 'There's a whole world out there . . .'

She felt her mind had expanded since she came here. Different place, different people. The reason for travel. And Bettine, she thought, smiling to herself, reminds me of that fidgety little filly I gave back to Liam because of all her shying and bolting and behaving like a woman. She had been repeating Paddy's words.

'Now, where have I heard that before?' Liam had said. 'You're becoming Paddy's mouthpiece. She's as quiet as a lamb with me.' Stupid beggar, she'd thought at the time, or something even worse.

It was a strange thing with horses; they made you talk rough. That was what she'd tried to convey to Liam; the steaming pungency and the farting around the loose boxes if you happened to go after they'd been fed. It didn't really suit her. Medieval history for a refined young lady with a French education would be much better. That was when she felt like her mother, understood her. But Liam's laugh, an all-over laugh, in his eyes, opening his mouth – he had fine teeth – throwing back his head . . . it was a fine thing about him, that laugh.

She was in a receptive frame of mind as she walked towards the cathedral. She would look round it and then have lunch outside at one of the cafés, before she drove back to Lapantelle. She remembered again the sight of those twin spires against the deep blue of the sky. Hadn't she been told by one of the teachers at Ste-Catherine's the words for the blue in the stained glass there? Ah, yes, *bleu de Chartres*. She would start with the outside, the wonderful doors. The interior deserved two full days.

She stood in front of the Right Bay for some time, letting her eyes travel along the carved figures with their large heads and disproportionately small bodies, reminding her, strangely, of the dwarves she had seen once in a travelling circus – sacred and profane, she thought, two sides of the same coin. When she'd been with the school, it had been a jaunt, now she could appreciate the full magnificence and power of the work of those early sculptors.

Then there were the flying buttresses, and she remembered when she had been there before, she had seen a teacher with her gaggle of pupils around her. Her French had been at times too swift to follow, but Nora had admired her skill in holding the children's attention, far better than their mademoiselle with the young ladies from Paris.

She had stood for a minute or two watching the teacher showing her pupils how to emulate the flying buttresses, facing each other in a row and making an arch with their arms, and she'd felt that niggle again. History. I'd like to study history at Trinity, medieval history, troubadors, ladies with wimples, knights on their destriers – she had seen paintings in the Cluny Museum. The thought came to her that Richard Trant had said it was the flying buttresses he wanted to see.

She walked round the side of the cathedral. It was such a glorious day that the interior could be left for another time. She felt dwarfed by the rearing walls as she stood near a family group, all looking skywards: mother, father, two boys, and a toddler who only wanted to explore.

'*Marcel*!' the mother shouted. '*Garde Raymond! Vite, vite!*' She watched with amusement one of the boys trying to get hold of his wriggling brother.

'Well, well! Nora, isn't it?' She turned, still smiling. It was Richard Trant. 'I had a premonition I'd see you here!' He was dressed casually in jeans and a tee shirt. He looked younger than she remembered him. Perhaps it was the clothes.

'Richard Trant!' She wasn't embarrassed. 'Well, we bumped into each other after all!' Nor did she feel any surprise, simply that it was a pleasure to meet him again.

He insisted that they should have lunch together and she accepted his invitation with pleasure also. Their meeting was a further addition to her new lifestyle; the drive into the nearest town, Chartres, to do some shopping, coffee with a friend, meeting an acquaintance *par hazard*, that's how it went. She was as much at ease as had it been Liam.

Her mind stayed on Liam while Richard Trant was having a consultation with the waiter about a particular Loire wine he wanted. So pleasant. Although she was always at ease with Liam, he'd kissed her only on rare occasions, Christmas or parties Paddy gave celebrating a win, but there was always an assumed nonchalance on his part which was difficult to break, also a sternness in the set of his features when he wasn't laughing. Was it a warning to her? This is serious for me. Don't pretend anything you don't feel. But hadn't she played the part of the boss's daughter for all she was worth, standing by Paddy's side, receiving with him the congratulations, instead of aligning herself with the young people laughing and talking amongst themselves?

There had been that time – she'd thought about it often – when she and Liam had been sitting in the woods while their horses grazed and there had been a sudden silence between them. He'd turned to her and put his arms round her roughly and said, 'Oh, Nora . . .' She had seen his eyes, brimming, hot, and known he wasn't joking. She could feel him trembling against her, and she had remained very still as if any movement would make it worse.

Then she had said, imitating him, but laughing, 'Oh, Liam!' pulling a face, and he'd flung himself away from her and sat silently for a minute, head down, before he'd jumped up and gone over to the horses.

'Are you coming?' he'd grudgingly asked. She had felt abashed, debased by her own triviality . . .

'Are you installed in your house now?' she heard Richard Trant say. 'Sensible *sommelier*, that. And I think you'll like the sole meunière. They know what they're talking about.' He looked around the large dining room, a man who liked to do things well if it's being appreciated. Earlier, she had said that a *croque-monsieur* at a café would do.

'Yes, I am,' she said. 'It needs a lot doing to it, but I'll take my time.'

'Have you lots of time?' he asked her, smiling.

'Yes, I have, as it happens.'

'No anxious parents hovering?'

'My mother lives in Phoenix, Arizona. And she has never hovered.' Quite the contrary, but she didn't want to confide in him already.

He waited until the waiter had poured their wine and gone away. He raised his glass to her as he asked, 'And your father?'

'He's dead,' she said, her face stony. 'What about yours?'

'Hale and hearty.'

'And your wife and children?' She sipped her wine, her eyes on him, all the savoir faire in the world. Lapantelle and her new lifestyle must be rubbing off already.

His face narrowed, and his eyes. He looked at her with a closed face, as he replied, 'What a boring subject this is. Family. Leave it.' He made a gesture with his hands, as if brushing crumbs away. His eyes changed swiftly, now they were on her, smiling, frank. 'I wanted to tell you how much you impressed me that time at Chantilly. You looked sad. As if you weren't with us.'

She smiled a false, dawning smile. 'And that's a great imagination you have there, Mr Trant!' Then she changed it to the one Liam had said would break anyone's heart. She was so sure of herself.

'I have to have. I'm an architect.'

'Ah, yes, I was forgetting. Well, you'd be interested in my little house. It's dwarfed by the ground around it, as if it's occupying something else's place.'

'That's probably what it *is* doing. Something that was knocked down or fell down or was burned down.' She remembered Bettine's remark. 'Very interesting,' he said, professionally. 'If you don't like it, you could build a larger one in its place. I could help you.'

She laughed at him. 'You're what we call a fast worker. But it's a right nice little house and will do me well for my French holidays, but—'

'Your heart's in Ireland?' She *had* been laying on the Irish brogue a bit.

'Well, yes it is. Yes . . .' She'd give it up, this posing.

He was a good companion, sophisticated, knowledgeable, charming. After lunch they spent a couple of hours in the cathedral and he was knowledgeable about the stained glass windows and how they were a kind of learning aid that taught the scriptures with a bit of astrology and shareholding thrown in, judging by the coats of arms of the many wealthy families who had helped.

It was the introduction of the flying buttresses which had enabled them to get rid of unpierced walls, he told her, and proceeded to explain it much in the same way as the French teacher she had seen years ago. 'They fascinate me,' he added. 'Always have.'

'I was hopeless at mathematics, but I'm getting the hang of it.'

'I'll give you another lesson any time you like.' His eyes were on her, adult eyes, making her aware that twenty-three against this man's sophistication was probably young.

But she enjoyed being with him. She felt holiness creeping over her as he made her see the cathedral's beauty.

She said, 'I thought of coming to mass here on Sunday. Light a candle for . . .' She stopped.

'I wanted to do that too, although I'm not a Catholic, but I've got to get back to Paris that morning. There's a house I've to look over for the firm.'

'What a pity,' she said, and was disappointed. Or discomfited?

He had an architect's eye and wanted to see the view of the old town from the Bishop's Palace – he insisted on calling it that although it was now a museum – and led her down the terrace from the garden so that they could get a view of the old town. 'A gem,' he said, enthusiastically. 'Down there the original town, up here a city within a city. I could spend weeks here.' His interest was genuine.

They wandered about in the old town looking at the houses, and when the summer heat tired them, chose a table in a converted mill and had a drink. He pointed out the *tertres*, the steps leading up again to the modern town.

'You could draw the plan,' he said. 'The cathedral on the hill, the old town at its foot which has evolved on the Eure. Charming. So satisfying. Sixteenth century.'

They leant on a stone wall at the river and looked as people do at rivers, and time slid past in the same way. She felt the heat on her back as well as the lingering warmth from the Loire wine.

She was beginning to be excited by his presence, a strange, new feeling. On the surface, he was courteous and informative, but his eyes seemed to hold hers longer than was necessary, adult eyes, questioning, stirring, so that she had to look away.

'Sixteenth century,' he said again. 'Do you see the protruding first floor, like a gallery . . .' The words seemed to cover other words.

She was not surprised when he said, 'Are you going to take pity on a poor traveller and take me to see your house now?' Questioning eyes.

'I'm sorry,' she said as if she had prepared her answer already, 'I have another engagement.' Her words hid different ones. Like, why not?

'Oh!' He looked taken aback, slightly unbelieving, as if she couldn't possibly have engagements already. Or be refusing him. 'Tomorrow?' His smile had no mirth in it.

'What a pity,' she said. 'Only this morning I made arrangements with a friend to spend the day with her. We're shopping for my house. Such a sweet girl, Bettine. And she has another friend who'll help me . . .' She overdid the explanations in the relief of telling the truth for a change. What had made her refuse? Was it the sight of the two spires floating above them as if tethered. The sacred and profane?

'I'm so very sorry, Nora.' He turned towards her and took her hands. 'Are you fobbing me off?'

She could have wept. This would have been the very man. 'I don't know what you mean?' She looked away from him, trying to be nonchalant.

'Can I book you in advance, then? You seem to be a very popular young lady. I intend coming here again next weekend.'

'Do you?'

'I'm really intrigued by your house. We could have lunch in Chartres on Saturday, then I could drive you home.'

'I have a car.' He burst out laughing.

'Then, may I follow you home? I promise I shan't stay long. I'm a very busy man, you know.'

She was thinking as he spoke. They would be back at her house between three and four. It would be quite light.

'I'll have to drive up to Paris that night. I've drawings to complete, but I'd love to have a look at your property.' He imprisoned her with his eyes.

She gave in. She must stop behaving like a schoolgirl. 'Why not?' she said. Aloud.

Later, when she was driving back to Lapantelle she wondered if it was Paddy's influence which had made her behave as she did. He'd been critical of most young men, always tried to warn her about the 'bad boyos' around. Once he'd said, 'We're all bad boyos.'

They had shaken hands at the car park and she'd thanked him for her lunch. 'You said that very prettily,' he said. 'Irish education must be good.'

'Paris,' she said, and thought she must sound younger than twenty-three to boast like that. She was right. She had to get about more. Well, yes, but . . . she hadn't liked his eyes.

Six

Nora's visit to Denise Pernet's emporium, Bettine's friend, was entirely satisfactory. The shop was stocked with all kinds of furnishings for the home, and she found the owner's taste, fortunately, very much in accordance with her own.

Denise was a tall blonde young woman, immaculately made-up and so smartly dressed that Nora felt at first rather bowled over by her elegance. But underneath the surface sophistication, she soon found there was a friendly young woman with a genuine interest in her and in trying to help. She came away feeling pleased with her purchases; the sign of a good saleswoman.

She had ordered an occasional table, a comfortable sofa with plenty of cushions in exotic fabrics and colours, elegant lampshades, and one or two vases for the flowers she hoped to grow.

Bettine had accompanied her and when Nora suggested they should come to Lapantelle some evening, they both agreed: Bettine with enthusiasm, Denise quieter, but seeming equally pleased. This is what I need in my life, Nora thought, the company of women.

And she was also becoming used to her own company, and even liking it. She gave the house a thorough cleaning, washing curtains and bed covers, scrubbing the kitchen floor – a job she actually liked – and when the two girls arrived a few days later in Denise's smart coupé, they were loud in their praise. At least Bettine was, Denise was more muted.

They discussed where the various pieces should be placed – they had arrived by carrier the day before – over a meal which Nora had prepared with as much expertise as she could summon, remembering Mhairi's tuition and, with the help of some good wine, they chattered animatedly together.

Denise approved of the furniture placing in the small sitting room. 'So right the sofa facing the fire and the coffee table in front of it. I can just see you having cosy evenings in winter there, mademoiselle. This is a room for relaxation, for *le four o'clock*, for conversing with someone you like, or retiring to when it rains. And the gold silk lampshade behind so that the light falls on the occupants of the sofa . . .' She sighed with pleasure. 'And a fire in that lovely fireplace, unusual enough to have come from some chateau . . . Are you expecting many visitors, mademoiselle?'

'Or boyfriends?' Bettine asked.

'Neither,' Nora laughed. 'I imagine I'll go back to Ireland when I have this place in order. My father left the house to me when he died, and there are things to do there.' She found she was able to say that without the usual sadness.

The two young Frenchwomen were impressed. 'Of course, an heiress will have absolutely no difficulty in finding suitors wherever she is,' Bettine commented. 'If you haven't found one already?'

Nora laughed. 'I'm not in any hurry.'

Denise nodded approval. 'It's best to be busy about one's own affairs. Fortunately, my shop occupies all my time.'

'The men in Ireland would soon change all that if they saw you,' Nora said.

Denise shook her head. 'What is your proverb? "Once bitten, twice shy" is it not? I am a divorcée and now I am very cautious – I don't want to make the same mistake twice.

51

Bettine doesn't believe me.' She laughed at her. 'She is in love. I don't want to spoil her rosy dreams.'

'No, you're right,' Nora agreed. 'It must be agreeable to be so obviously happy.'

Before they left they painted a word picture for her of the surrounding countryside. 'So charming, the Loire Valley. So *douce*. True France.'

'And so many beautiful houses to see,' Bettine agreed. 'Château Maintenon, for instance. You mustn't miss it. It was a love nest for our king, Louis the Fourteenth.'

They were on first name terms when the two girls got into Denise's coupé parked outside the gates. 'You are not afraid here?' Bettine asked her.

'Why should she be?' Denise said. 'Those gates can keep people out as well. Besides, there's another house there.' She had noticed the guest cottage.

'It's unoccupied at present,' Nora said, and wished now, with darkness around her, that there had been someone in it. But she waved vigorously to the departing coupé. The Leroux couple were just around the corner, barely two minutes away, she reminded herself. But on the other side of the huge gates . . .

She washed up after they had gone with determined cheerfulness. She had made two good friends. They had exchanged telephone numbers and she could ring them at any time. Denise had said to drop in at her shop for a coffee when she was in Chartres and Bettine would arrange another meeting soon.

When she went to bed she slept heavily until three in the morning when she suddenly awoke with her mind full of Paddy. But he's dead, she told herself, you have to accept it. You're doing well, you've made friends here, and you've met Richard Trant. Now, he's experienced, charming, he would make you forget . . . she drifted off again.

When she awoke about eight with the sun streaming in the wide window, she felt cheerful and optimistic and ready to face the day.

Fortunately, Monsieur Leroux called that morning and declared he was ready to start, which he did vigorously under Nora's instructions. The following afternoon, Tuesday, he went with her to Chartres market where they loaded the car with shrubs, flowers for planting and vegetable plants and seeds.

They soon established an easy relationship. He was, she thought, in his middle thirties and much more approachable than his wife. He told her he worked for a farmer nearby and he could give her time in between the farmer's demands. They had no family, he said cheerfully – a man who accepted his lot.

He studied Nora's plan intently and declared himself pleased with it. She had bought a white marker to indicate where the beds should go, and when she saw that he was into his stride, she tackled the plot he had dug for her at the back of the house, her vegetable garden. First, a special place for the herbs they had bought: coriander, basil, thyme, rosemary, fennel, chives, parsley. Lettuce seeds would be strewn amongst the vegetables. If it was too late for potatoes, there was always next year.

When he was helping her with the vegetable planting, she discussed the patio with him and fortunately he knew just the man for the job. Pleased, she said she would pay another visit to Chartres and buy a patio table and chairs, along with a garden umbrella. He was that rare find in a gardener, a man who encouraged her in her enthusiasm, and was prepared to work towards its conclusion.

She realized she was like Paddy. Once, he had said to her, 'You and I are just the same when we get the bit between our teeth.'

She was so busy for the rest of that week that she hadn't any time to visit Château Maintenon's love nest which Bettine had recommended, and she was so tired at night that she slept soundly, thankfully without dreaming.

Monsieur Leroux, more communicative than his wife, dropped a brick one day. 'Madame Clancy generally arrives about this time,' he said.

'Who?' she asked.

'The madame who occupies the house at the gates. She comes to paint. She goes off in her car, but sometimes she sets up her easel in the garden. Perhaps she won't come now since you are here?'

'No, it's her own property. My mother left it to her.' She was becoming so well-adjusted that she felt slightly annoyed at his news.

'That is fortunate for her. And there is a son and two daughters. Sometimes they come also.'

'Really?' Life was full of surprises, she thought.

On Friday, the day before she had to meet Richard Trant for lunch, she had a surprising letter from Liam. It read:

Dear Nora,

I had your postcard from Paris, and aren't you the lucky one swanning about there and you with a ready tongue in their language as well.

We're all fine here. My mother looks after the house, but she's a bit unsettled, I'm thinking. I keep to my own flat. She talks about keeping house for an old uncle nearby who's not so well, but to tell you the truth, I don't see that much of her. I'm pretty busy running the place and trying to keep everything in order for you coming back.

The horse we trained for Colonel Moore had a win at Leopardstown and we're taking it around to give it some experience. It's being noticed, judging by the stakes.

I've been wondering how you like your new inheritance and can just see you whipping it into shape. You're a great worker when you get started. I've seen you around the yard, although you say you don't like it, busy with the yard brush and quite bossy with the lads. Bred in the bone, but the charm goes with it.

Now, I'm afraid I'm going to let you down. You remember I promised Paddy I'd look after the place for you for a time, but unfortunately, or fortunately, I've been offered a fine post with a Dublin firm, too good to refuse.

They're willing to wait until I get things fixed up here, and I've got the names of two good men who would be willing to take over from me, well recommended. And I wouldn't leave, of course, until you were back here and you tried them out and the place was running as well as you wanted it. I'd give you proper notice and all that sort of thing.

I'm sad indeed. You know how I followed my dad about the place when I was a lad, but since I've grown up, much as I love the horses, I've never felt it could be my life's work. I remembered him saying, 'Liam, find what you want to do then do it with all your might.'

It isn't the horses that are at fault, although I have a great love of them and that's bred in the bone as well. No, it's the people that follow them, the narrowness of their vision. Paddy was a prototype, horses and women, and I hope you don't mind me saying that.

I found myself becoming bored with the one topic all the time – nothing so trivial as your la-de-da dislike of the smell around the stables – and a wish to enlarge my mind with other things – more important things to me –

and I've found that in surveying. It absorbs me, widens my appreciation of the land we live in and other lands and – that may be the nub of it – I want to see other places, see how other people live.

I'm getting on, twenty-three, just like you, and I've never been anywhere but race tracks. You, at least, have lived in another country, seen other people. Your mother wanted something different also, but being her she made the mistake of choosing Flannagan. Still, it got her away. She was a sad woman. I could see that.

There was another reason why I wanted my independence far from your father's place, but that's gone now. I'd thought since I was in short trousers, that there was nobody like Paddy Malone's daughter, and still think it, but you've made it pretty plain you're not interested. I think sometimes of that haughty look of yours as if I was an insect about to crawl over you, then that thought is cancelled by remembering your smile, that heartbreaking smile of yours. And, as if that wasn't enough, there's your hair, as if it had taken its colour from the copper beech in the paddock lane . . . I'm making a fool of myself now, so I'll stop.

When you come home, I'll be here and I'll have the accounts ready and give you notice, all right and proper. And I shan't leave until you're fixed up with someone you like to run the place.

You'll see Marchmount isn't in the red and you still have a roof over your head in Ireland. Don't tell me you don't miss it at times. I know you too well.

I send you my true love, Liam.

Seven

Saturday was humid, the sun obliterated behind a haze, and the two spires of the cathedral merely shimmered on the horizon as Nora drove into Chartres to meet Richard Trant.

She had chosen her dress with care and elected to wear the one she had worn at Chantilly, a two-piece of patterned voile, the dress with strapped shoulders and a fluted skirt. It seemed cool enough for the day and smart enough for the occasion.

Her hair had been pinned up while she was working in the garden, but now she let it hang loose about her face and peered at herself in the mirror through it. She tossed her head like a prancing pony and saw it swing behind her shoulders because of its weight. The light from the window lit up its copper richness and she nodded at her reflection, saying, 'Yes, well, yes. Will that please you, Mr Trant?'

He was waiting for her in front of the cathedral where they had arranged to meet. Again, she got a pleasant shock to see how good-looking he was, how suave. Liam had an awkward coltish charm which was attractive. He was awkward, possibly because he hadn't quite reached that suavity he was aiming for, but his attractiveness had taken him from a boyish shyness to a young man who wasn't worldly yet, but was quite aware of his appeal to females, although was doing his best to hide that awareness.

'How cool you look today, Nora,' Richard Trant said, cool also and smiling as they shook hands. 'I like the gossamer look. You women are lucky compared with men.' He was wearing linen trousers with a loose white shirt and looked as cool as she felt, as cool as his attitude.

He, she thought, was the right age, the pinnacle that Liam was aiming for. Being with Richard Trant was being with the kind of man that made women envy you. She would have to be careful to hide her pleasure.

'I had to get out of my work clothes to appear in public,' she said. 'I've been doing a great deal at my cottage since we last met.'

'You're going to show me that later,' he said, 'but meantime, where would you like to go for lunch?'

'Somewhere outside, please.'

'Would you like to drive out of Chartres, say to Illiers? It's quieter, and you could say you'd been where Proust lived.' She was hazy about Proust.

'It would be cool by the river here, don't you think, in the old town?' She had formed an attachment to it.

'Fine by me. I have my car parked here. Where's yours?'

'Not far away, but let's walk. It's downhill.'

'But uphill all the way.' He laughed.

She thought it sounded like a quotation.

They set off and the little wind that blew as they descended the steep streets, stirred her voile skirt and made her feel feminine, like that picture she'd seen of the goddess of spring, Persephone, was it? Well, near enough.

He drew her attention to an inn sign, in wrought iron, of a man in period dress sitting at a table tackling a roast pig, and they laughed and said it was too hot for that. Then, she pointed out to him a house with the shutters painted with trompe l'œil images of geraniums in pots. It would be good to see it from the inside when they were shut. Could she adapt the idea? She would mention it to Denise.

'I have shutters on my cottage,' she said to Richard Trant, 'but I never close them.'

'Aren't you afraid? All the French do.'

'No, it's too claustrophobic for me. Besides I'm not easily scared.'

'Don't you think that it depends what it is?'

'What do you mean?'

'Well, say it was something which really surprised you. Something you least expected.'

She looked at him and met his eyes. They disturbed her. Why was that?

'I'm not timid,' she said. She dismissed his remark with a laugh. That was the difference between thirty-five (if that was what he was) and twenty-three. You could be discomfited more easily.

They settled down eventually in a good-looking restaurant by the river where they had the advantage of shade from the trees on the bank. Now she felt at ease with him again as they found a table. It was busy and they were surrounded by other people laughing and talking. It was always easier outside. If you ran out of words you could comment on the view. 'Lovely,' she said. 'I could sit here for ever.'

'Have a look at the menu.' He gave her an indulgent smile and held up his hand for a waiter.

She was happy being there. Where every prospect pleases, she thought.

They talked a lot and ate and drank a fair amount, and then they had leisurely coffees. Everybody seemed to be doing the same. The restaurant remained busy.

He was generous. 'Light wine seduces you,' he said. (She wasn't sure if it was the same bottle.) 'You think it will never go to your head, but at least it loosens your tongue.'

Hers more than his, she thought. She had talked a lot about Marchmount, about her mother in Arizona, about Paddy and how comfortable she and he had been with each other, and then he had died. 'It was too good to last,' she said. 'Such happiness.'

'You still miss him?' His eyes were steel grey and as piercing as a rapier, like a psychiatrist or what she thought of as a psychiatrist. She'd never met one.

'Oh, yes, I miss him. But being here has been a welcome break. It's given me something else to think about, and when I go back there will be a lot of arrangements to be made. Liam, who's been with us nearly all his life and mine, is going off for a land surveyor.' She saw his puzzled expression and laughed. 'That's our way of talking. You get used to it. And I want to persuade him to stay.'

'You think he will?'

'He's fond of the place; grew up in it.' She tossed her head, caught his look.

'Well, good luck.' A bit of a sneer there? 'I've been in Dublin,' he continued, 'at an architects' conference. I stayed in the Shelbourne.'

'Is there anywhere else?' she said.

'You little snob.' He laughed.

'Oh, I didn't mean it like that.' She was mortified. 'I meant it literally. All the county balls and such are held there and Paddy always asked me to go with him.'

'Who's Paddy?'

'The Paddy I've been telling you about. My father . . . I called him that after Mother left us. I thought it would give him a little comfort, you know. He was badly needing it. There was only me.'

'Hadn't . . .?' He hesitated. 'I don't know how to put this delicately. Hadn't he anywhere else to go, like a friend of his own age?'

60

She blushed, spoiling the coolness. She felt the heat under her arms, not at all what she wanted. 'You don't understand. He was going all over the place, Paddy. There were heaps of people, but I went with him. Oh, he had quite an eye for the girls, so had Liam, but he hadn't the joking way Paddy had with them. Not that I minded either of them flirting about . . . We're great flirts, you know. So was I, Paddy Malone's daughter; everyone knew me at the races . . . Anyhow, this is all about me. What about you?'

'Oh, I don't have nearly such an interesting life as you. You'd be bored to tears . . .' He looked around. 'Shall we go?'

She was rebuffed and looked at her watch to hide it. 'Goodness, it's four o'clock! The Irish can talk the hind legs off a donkey.' She laughed what she hoped was a trilling sort of laugh and got up. She had a horrible feeling that the voile was stuck between her legs at the back, or worse, and excused herself and went to the Ladies . . . but it wasn't.

They walked back to his car and as they passed the cathedral he asked her if she would like to go in.

'No, thank you,' she said. 'I'll have other opportunities.' But she was not in the mood. 'I'll get my car now . . . It's round the back. It was so busy.'

'You did promise that I could see your house, Nora.' He sounded anxious. 'Is the offer still on?'

She feigned surprise. 'Did I? Well, of course, if you'd like to, I don't mind.'

'That's sweet of you. Architects are curious creatures.' His smile was utterly charming. 'When you appear with your car at the front there, I'll fall in behind you. OK?'

'OK.'

He turned towards the doors of the cathedral. 'Beautiful,' he said, 'aren't they? How lucky you are to have a house nearby. Cathedrals should be like bus stations. Drop in when you like.'

Nora suddenly changed her mind. 'Shall we go in for a few minutes? I feel the same as you do.'

'Sure.'

When they were inside, she spoke severely to herself. Calm down. You can't do anything else but that, in this holy place. Be at peace with yourself. This is a perfectly nice, youngish man, sophisticated, from London, likely. There is no need to feel . . . apprehensive. Paddy used to say to you, putting on the brogue a bit, 'You get some quaire ideas in that little head of yours . . .'

When she looked at Richard Trant his head was lowered.

He followed her in his car and stayed steadily a few yards behind until they reached the gates. She saw immediately that there was another car there. She jumped out and met him. 'Park alongside mine, Richard. I wasn't expecting anyone else to be here. Never mind, there's plenty of room.'

'Right. These are the gates? Yes, you're right, they're huge.' She let him open them and they walked through. He closed them carefully. 'Do you lock them?'

'Only at night. We just walk across the lawn from here. Better with a drive. You can't call it a lawn, but you'll see where I'm having beds made.'

'Yes, good idea.'

She was looking at the guest cottage as they passed and she noticed the shutters were open, also the door. If she had been alone, she would have knocked and introduced herself. She felt suddenly pleased. She was making a new life for herself. Now there was a new person coming into it, Madame Clancy, as Monsieur Leroux had said. All the better. She was quite independent, an owner, an employer of labour; an heiress, Bettine and Denise had called her.

She would show this Richard Trant what she had done to improve the cottage and then he'd go off to Paris. Probably she wouldn't see him again. And perhaps later on she would call on Mrs Clancy and offer some help: milk, sugar, tea and the like. It would be good to have her there, in the guest cottage.

Eight

'Let's have a cup of tea first,' Nora said when they were in the small hall. They were forced to stand close to each other and it made her feel nervous. But then, she had to face it, she was out of her usual milieu here, a different country, different people. Being a heiress didn't seem to make a damned bit of difference.

'Lead on Macduff,' he said, smiling down at her.

She went ahead of him into the kitchen. 'This is the kitchen,' she said unnecessarily.

'A good living space, honest, that's the main thing.' He indicated the two easy chairs in front of the television at the other end of the room.

'I can keep my eyes on the pots boiling,' she said lightly. She threw her voile jacket on a chair, trying to appear at ease. Hadn't she come to the conclusion that she needed experience? Here was a golden opportunity, alone with a man of some sophistication. 'Please sit down.'

'A grand table,' he said, pulling out a chair.

'Honest?' She smiled at him. 'An honest table.'

'I hate poky ones. Some of my best work has been done at kitchen tables.'

'Where do you live?' she said as she filled the kettle.

'London. Holborn, or did.' He was terse. 'I have a roving commission with my firm. I'm not dependent on anyone. I have no need of a permanent address.'

64

'So, no commitments?' She could say anything with her back to him.

'You only have commitments if you allow them to happen. I've had enough of that . . . Good view to the back as well, I should imagine,' he said. 'Are the bedrooms there?'

'Yes, two, and there's an attic one. And I have a proper sitting room on the other side of the hall. I've tried to make it more comfortable and attractive, a drawing room, really.' They had one on a huge scale at Marchmount with a conservatory off it. Paddy had called it the orangerie as a joke.

'Perhaps we'll withdraw to it later,' he said, and when she put the teapot on the table she met his eyes. They were expressionless, they didn't match the teasing remark.

'Perhaps. Do you take sugar or milk?'

'Neither. A man of few indulgences. What's the French for afternoon tea?'

'*Le four o'clock.*'

He raised his eyebrows. 'Ask a stupid question . . . Sit down, Nora. You're making me nervous.' He pulled out a chair for her. 'You look flushed. It's hot, isn't it? Thundery. I feel it, too.'

She wished she looked as cool as he did. She sat down opposite him. They both sipped their tea. When she lifted her eyes she found his on her.

'You have a rare kind of beauty. Did you know that?' Calculating eyes. Not warm. 'Not the usual English cream and roses.'

'But then I'm Irish.' She relaxed as if she'd scored a point. And then, changing the subject, she said, 'I got quite a surprise to see that other car there. But I know my mother left the guest cottage to a friend of hers.'

'Strange. Do you know anything about this friend?'

'Just that they were at school together in Paris, my school, but nothing after that. She'll be in her forties, like my mother. Her name is Clancy. Mrs Clancy.'

'You know a lot. Anything else?'

'Only what the gardener tells me. She's a painter. It will be quite nice to have her there.'

He had got up and was wandering about the room as if he'd lost interest. The light had darkened and there was an ominous roll of thunder, seemingly quite near.

He held up a forefinger. 'See. What did I say? In for a spot of trouble. Are you afraid?'

'I don't like it.' When it had rumbled about Dublin Bay and rolled in their direction, she had run into Paddy's arms when she was small. 'Here comes Brian Boru to get you!' he'd say and cuddle her close.

Richard Trant was now examining the door, running his hand over it. Very much at ease, but wasn't that the kind of man she wanted to meet now? 'Lovely old wood. Quite a lot earlier than the fabric of the house. It's possible that if there was a house here before, it could have been removed from it. I thought I saw some signs of foundations when we were walking across your lawn, a bump here and there.'

'That's interesting.' This was an intelligent conversation. She felt relieved.

'Have you seen your solicitor yet?'

'No. I've been too busy.'

'He could tell you.' His words were almost drowned by a much louder sound of thunder, more a clap than a rumble.

'That was near,' she said, swallowing. 'No, I haven't seen . . .' Another clap like a ghostly audience in the wings made her draw her breath sharply. She said hurriedly, 'If you want to have a look round outside, we'd better do it now in case it rains.' And then he might leave.

'You aren't afraid?' he smiled.

'Of course not. But I think we'd better . . .' She got up.

When they got to the door, he put an arm round her. 'Not to worry. And thanks for the tea. You're sweet, entertaining me like this. I appreciate it.'

Relief flooded her. He was going. 'It's nothing.' She shrugged her shoulders and his arm fell away.

When they were outside there was another clap of thunder directly above them and a spot of rain fell on her bare head, a large splat rather than a spot.

'Oh, I forgot,' he said. 'I've got a house-warming present for you in my car. I'll just run and get it before the heavens open.'

'Please don't bother . . .' Just get away. The words trembled on the tip of her tongue but he had gone, striding swiftly over the grass. Calm down! She spoke sternly to herself. This is the experience you wanted, isn't it? Someone different from Liam. And now you're desperate to get rid of him . . .

He was back in a few seconds with an oblong cardboard box in his hand. 'Just a bottle of bubbly.'

'Oh, you shouldn't have done that,' she said accepting it. 'Thank you.' As she spoke the heavens did open, a solid sheet of water.

'Run for it!' he said, putting an arm round her.

They were only a yard or two from the cottage and they were back inside before they got wet. Through the waterfall of rain, she could see the door of the guest cottage, shut now, but there was no sign of anyone. Perhaps whoever it was had gone away. Perhaps someone, anyone, had chosen to park their car outside the gates. She would have so liked to catch a glimpse of Mrs Clancy, to wave to her, to beckon her to come on over, as the Americans said.

'Well, that settles it,' Richard Trant said, smiling. 'I shall have to stay the night.'

'What a hope!' she said cheekily. Strangely enough, she

was now in command of the situation; the way she felt when she managed to calm down a fractious horse she was riding. It's all a question of technique, she thought. I've got the hang of him now. He's mischievous. He likes to tease, but there's no harm in him, really. He's only passing the time with me because he's bored with life and possibly unhappy. I bet he's left his wife, or she's left him . . .

'Do you mean you'd turn me out into the storm, have me catch my death of cold?'

They were close together in the small hall, too close, and she said hurriedly, 'Well, since you've been so generous, I'll get two glasses and we can toast my house. Go into the sitting room, please.'

'Brilliant idea.' He took the bottle from her. His eyes were those of someone who had scored a point.

In the kitchen, reaching to a cupboard for the glasses, she glanced at her watch and saw it was five o'clock. The darkness outside made it seem much later. She'd thought he'd be on his way by that time. Why was she so unsure of herself when he was around? What was she afraid of? She'd never been in a situation when she had felt so much apprehension, and yet it was totally unfounded. Or was it? He was . . . unfathomable, it was difficult to tell if he was joking or not.

When she went into the room, he was seated on the sofa in front of the fireplace with the opened bottle on the table in front of him.

'You'll see I'm making myself at home.' He smiled round at her. 'Come and sit beside me.' She put down the glasses and sat, not too close. 'A charming little room,' he said. 'Just right for withdrawing. Small, but the fireplace redeems it.'

'Thank you,' she said. And again, when he gave her a generous glass of champagne.

'Your manners are impeccable,' he said. 'I can't imagine

you being anything but a lady, and yet . . . I knew someone who was always a lady. But underneath . . .' He clinked glasses with her, smiling.

Nora sipped. 'Lovely champagne.'

'Quite a connoisseur, are you? What was I saying?'

'You were talking about ladies.'

'Well, to hell with all ladies. Let's have a toast instead to your cottage. What have you called it?'

'It had a name, Le Manoir.'

'That clinches it, you're on a grand site at least.'

She thought of saying, 'You should see Marchmount,' but luckily, didn't.

She had learned early from Paddy the tonic effect of champagne. He thought it a more ladylike drink for her when they had guests, although they always had a nightcap before going to bed.

The rain had settled into a torrential downpour, and it was so dark that she reached behind her and clicked on the lamp. They were immediately in an intimate pool of golden light. It was comforting, a good way of passing a miserable afternoon, and once he had left, if the rain had abated, she'd go across the lawn to the guest cottage and see if the Clancys were really there. This was a fine life, as different as chalk from cheese from the one she'd had with Paddy. Much more varied. Yes. . .

'You're not going to get rid of me.' Richard Trant laughed, looking out of the window. 'I'm a prisoner now.'

'It won't last,' she said. 'You'll soon get off.' It sounded a bit brusque, but she was a woman of the world, well-used to entertaining a man in a thunderstorm in her own little drawing room.

Paddy had valued good manners, and so had Ste-Catherine's. 'Would you like me to put on the electric fire?' she said.

'Good idea. You think of everything.'

She laughed and bent forward to press the switch. I'm setting it up like an assignation, for God's sake. Veuve Cliquot Vintage, she noticed on the label of the champagne bottle. Paddy's choice. In the golden light from behind them, Richard Trant looked very handsome, the aquiline features, the thin but finely-shaped mouth. Liam's charm lay in the broad openness of his face, of his smile, the slightly snub nose, the wide grin. What you see is what you get. She looked at the grey curtain of rain, solid as gunmetal. She felt the arm along the back of the sofa, now it was resting on her shoulders. The golden glow of the lamp combined with the golden glow inside her from the champagne, was seductive.

He topped up her glass, and with the gesture, she remembered Paddy saying, whiskey bottle in his hand, 'Ah, come on, now, another one for the road.'

'Thank you,' she said, lifting the glass, putting her lips to it and putting it down again. 'Have you heard from your mother since Chantilly?'

He shook his head dismissively. 'We don't correspond much. You've got to watch mothers. They try to barge in, offer advice when they haven't a clue, out of their class. It's only those who are in the middle of it who know . . .' He sounded bitter.

'I don't have that trouble,' she said, 'my mother being in Arizona.' She didn't mind the arm, did she now, but the hand, she'd have to watch that hand which was lingering near the strap of her dress. Suddenly she was stone cold sober. This was an untenable situation she'd got herself into. 'It was fun meeting by chance in Chartres,' she said.

'Marvellous fun.' He was mocking her. She could feel a finger under her shoulder strap. 'I thought at Chantilly you were remote, off-hand, really. Now that you have told me

70

about your father, it puts quite a different complexion on things. You're lonely. You need company. You're searching for someone . . .'

She was puzzled. Should she take that remark sincerely, conjuring up as it did those cosy evenings at the hall fire with Paddy, or what Liam called a come-on? He'd been talking about a horse-mad or man-mad young girl who haunted the yard and gave everyone the come-on. She decided to take it sincerely.

'Life,' she said, 'with the exception of the three years spent at school in Paris, has been centred on Marchmount. That was my background, with Paddy. After my mother left, he and I were very close . . . We didn't have holidays, there were so many fixtures spread over the year. Paddy always said we'd take a cruise sometime but we never did. I see now, it was a mistake to be so tied. That's why I was glad to come here. My mother had felt trapped, possibly for a different reason, but I had a kind of bitterness against her, you know, for treating Paddy like that, and I tried to make it up to him. Paddy expected a lot of me . . .'

'Didn't you have a manager?' He sounded bored. 'Drink up. We've got to finish this bottle before I go away.'

She obediently sipped at her champagne, cheered at the thought that he was leaving. 'Now, I have. That's Liam. But before that, it was murder with them coming and going. Mother ran away with one of them.' That's what the champagne did to you. A little more made you say a little too much.

'Did she?' He sounded pleased. 'Well, maybe you've got a bit of a devil in you, too.' He smiled into her eyes.

'Not a chance.' Her shoulder suddenly felt bare. 'What the hell are you doing?' she said, relapsing into stable talk.

'Did your shoulder strap slip?'

'It did not.' She put it firmly back in its place. The trouble

71

with feeling ever so slightly tipsy was that conversation began to sound like a collection of non sequiturs. You lost track.

'So, you will have it all on your shoulders when you go back? Except for the faithful, bucolic Liam. Poor little rich girl! My god, you're lucky! If you knew what I've to pay out to a bitch who tricked me . . .'

'Mind your tongue!' She spoke as she would to Liam.

'Hey!' He turned and drew her against him. 'You can't get away with talking to me in that . . . autocratic way. You're all the same.'

'It comes naturally.' She pulled herself away. 'I'm used to speaking to the yard lads in the language they understand.' She breathed deeply. 'You haven't a clue what it's like to run a firm like ours. I tried to help, the accounts and so on . . .' She didn't know whether she was talking like this because of the champagne or because she was afraid. She sat straight. 'I really think you should go now, Richard. The rain's easing off.'

'Easing off, is it?'

'Paddy was the front man, of course. People expected him to be at every event where there was a horse trained by him. He was a presence. Liam used to say that. *He* had no time for appearing in public. He wants to be a land surveyor. Did I tell you that? I have to decide if I should ask him to stay on.' That was nonsense, of course. Liam's mind was made up. 'And then there's my wish to study medieval history . . .'

The force in his arms wasn't obvious, but she was again pressed back against the sofa cushions and his face came down on hers, his mouth stopping her talk. It was a hard mouth, and then there was his tongue . . . She tried to pull herself away from him and saw that both straps were off her shoulders.

'Did you do that?' She was furious. 'What the hell do you think you're doing?'

He looked at her, his mouth widening, lips closed, his eyes amused. 'You women. You amuse me. You really amuse me. The pretence, even the least expected of them . . .' His body was hard and bony; his sternum was boring into her soft breasts holding her imprisoned while he rapidly with one hand began to strip off his clothing and hers, imprisoning her with an iron arm while he did so.

She tried to scream, but he put a hand over her mouth and in terror she sunk her teeth into his hand.

'Bitch!' he said softly. 'You bloody bitch. I might have expected it.' His eyes were on her, reflective, cold.

'Please let me go.' She said it without shouting. 'This is stupid. Please let me go.'

'Let you go!' He feigned genuine astonishment. 'When you've been leading me on all day, blowing hot and cold. Did you think your money and your Paris connections would count? I'm prepared to be generous. I thought we understood each other.'

'You had better let me go.' She said it feigning weariness.

'Pleading now, are we? You struck me as a competent young woman; now you're just a little girl, Daddy's little girl.'

The room seemed a little lighter. 'The rain's easing off.'

'D'ye tell me that now?' She didn't like the imitation of the Irish brogue, nor the smile. He gripped her shoulders enough to hurt. 'I don't know what your father taught you, but I can well imagine, in your stately home, alone with him . . .'

She couldn't believe this. 'Will you take your hands off me!'

He smiled again, ignoring her. 'But didn't he tell you it was dangerous to behave like a teasing bitch?'

She felt sickened, mostly at herself. 'I find you,' she said, 'a patronising bugger.'

That smile again. Instead of having merely thin features,

73

they now seemed fox-like. Paddy had had a searchlight fixed up in the drawing room window so that they could watch the fox family gambolling on the lawn. That had been really joyous. This was not.

He forced her back again on the sofa. She tried kicking him, tried to aim at the place where it hurt most, but he seemed all sinew and bone, and as strong as a horse.

'A patronising bugger, is it?' She didn't recognize him now. 'Miss High and Mighty Irish heiress with her devoted Paddy and her lapdog Liam or whatever his bloody name is. It's time, my dear –' he was lying on top of her now, feeling naked – 'that you moved into the real world. If you won't play, you have to pay.' She opened her eyes and saw again that closed smile.

It was horrible and terrible. One of her arms was free. She swung it towards where the table was, and by a great stroke of luck her hand struck the neck of the bottle. Before he could stop her, she had emptied the Vintage Cliquot over his head. While he was cursing her, she was able to thump him good and hard with the bottle, and then, opening her mouth she screamed like a banshee or a leprechaun lost in its own strange world.

'You shouldn't have done that.' His quiet tone terrified her. Both hands gripped her arms. 'I've had a bad time, but someone has to pay for it. Since you were different, I was prepared to be lenient, treat it as a pleasant encounter . . .'

She opened her mouth again, filled her lungs and screamed, howled. As if in response, there was a heavy knocking at the door.

'It's Mrs Clancy's son!' she said. 'Probably the police with him . . .'

After that, she was hardly aware of what was happening except that his weight was no longer there. She heard the back door slam. She lay stunned for a second, but the

74

shouting was still going on: 'Miss Malone! Are you all right?'
A deep man's voice.

'Coming!' she shouted.

She lay stunned for a second or two, then braced herself,
pulled the torn voile dress up, adjusted the straps over her
shoulders, went to the door and opened it.

Standing there was a young man. 'Are you all right, Miss
Malone? We heard you screaming.'

'Quite all right. Do come in.' A lady had to be able to take
charge of any situation. It was called savoir faire.

Nine

His mother was on the veranda looking anxiously at them as Craig Clancy came across the lawn towards the guest cottage with Nora. 'I insisted on her coming, Robbie,' he said.

'I should hope so. Come along, my dear. Don't try to talk. What you need is a strong cup of coffee.' Americans were great believers in coffee, Nora remembered.

'I'm really all right,' she said, going up the steps towards the woman. 'Your son insisted . . .'

'Of course he did! And you're Laure Bouchier's daughter, of course.' She was leading Nora through the doorway, her arm round her shoulders, 'And you've met my son?'

'Yes. He's been very kind. You're both being very kind. I feel such a fool.' She felt she had to explain. 'You see, I had met this man once or twice, and I invited him in, and. . . .'

'Don't say another word. Just you sit there and relax.' They were in a large room, panelled in pine like a tennis pavilion, and Roberta Clancy ensconced Nora in a basket chair, well-padded with cushions. It was that kind of room, a place to relax in. There were similar chairs about and a sofa. 'I've got the coffee here. There's nothing better. I'm glad you shouted.' She smiled. 'You've got a good pair of lungs.'

Nora sipped the coffee Roberta Clancy had handed her. It was hot and strong and she felt immediately better. 'I'm being such a nuisance.'

'A nuisance! You'll hardly believe it, but Craig and I were just saying that we should ask you over for a drink when we heard you. We were dying to meet you.'

'You didn't think it would be like this!' She took another sip. It was surprising how her hands were trembling and her legs, behind the knees.

'Never mind. Well, well, Laure's daughter! Nora, isn't it? I can see the resemblance. You've got her look. Now, take your time. You must have had quite a shock.'

It was new to be called Laure's daughter. She had never thought of herself as anyone's daughter. Certainly, Laure hadn't bothered much about her. She met Craig Clancy's eyes. Did men feel embarrassed when one of their own sex was implicated? He smiled reassuringly at her. He was a reassuring kind of guy, that's how they said it. His looks were vaguely familiar.

Mrs Clancy, Roberta, Robbie, was talking away, possibly to put her at ease. 'Craig and I arrived at lunch time. You probably saw the car. It's nice to have him. I have two daughters as well, Lesley and Lois, both married. I can't get rid of this one.' She glanced affectionately at her son.

'She won't let me go, that's why. I'm just her lapdog, that's me. You're looking better now, Nora. I thought you were going to pass out when you opened the door to me.'

He had a puckish grin. Certainly not like his mother who was strong-featured, dark-eyed with strong dark brows, and had skin which looked as if it had been subjected to too much sun. Surprisingly, she had blonde hair. Nora had heard that some dark-haired women went blonde to cover incipient greyness. She had the same air of bandbox freshness which Nora had noticed in the American women who came to race meetings in Ireland.

'I'm very glad you held on to him,' Nora said. She wouldn't have believed that coffee was better than Paddy's

77

favourite tipple for all occasions, a stiff tot. 'I'm fine now,' she said, putting down her cup. 'Maybe I should just get back . . .' The embarrassment was back again. What a fool she'd been, letting herself get into such a situation!

'You'll do no such thing,' Mrs Clancy said. 'You're not fit to go back yet. Would you like to lie down here for an hour or so?'

'No, really, I'm fine. I've felt much worse when I've been thrown from a horse!' She steeled herself. 'You'll be thinking I'm pretty feeble to kick up such a row, shouting . . .'

'It couldn't have been for nothing. That's good enough for us.'

'She's right,' her son said. 'Take your time.' The puckish grin. 'Bit of an excitement for us.'

'I feel I should explain.' Her terror had gone. Not the trembling. She clasped her hands in her lap. 'I met this man in Paris, then I ran into him in Chartres again. He's an architect. He said he'd like to see my house . . .'

'And you made a mistake,' Mrs Clancy said. 'It's easily done.'

'If the rain hadn't started, and the thunder; it gave him an excuse to stay.' She clasped her hands tightly. 'And he'd given me a bottle of champagne . . . and somehow one thing led to another . . .' She stopped, imagining the scene again, feeling trapped, knowing she had been partly to blame, and then the utter terror and how she had filled her lungs and let the shout rip. As Mrs Clancy said, she had a good pair of lungs.

And would she ever forget that raised head, his alarmed eyes, like a fox alerted, the weight of his body suddenly removed, the scuffling noise of him dressing, the door slamming. A bad dream. A nightmare.

'Where were you?' Mrs Clancy asked. Her voice sounded almost peremptory.

'Where?' Strange question. 'In the little sitting room on the right side of the hall.'

'But that was a bedroom!' Her eyes widened, she looked puzzled, more than that, alarmed.

'Not now.'

'Does it matter, Mom?' Craig said. 'What does matter is, where the devil did he get to so quickly?'

'I'm sorry,' she said. 'I don't know what's come over me . . .' She passed her hand over her forehead. 'It used to be a bedroom. I got muddled. Didn't you see him at all, Craig?'

'I have a vague recollection now of a shadow rather than a figure streaking for the gates. But I was too intent on getting in.'

'You'd be right. I heard the noise of a car starting up. He'll be gone now.' Her reaction still seemed odd to Nora. Now she seemed to be someone who was gathering herself together. 'Anyhow, we'll tell it all to the police when we phone. These incidents are getting a bit too frequent nowadays.'

'Mom's on her hobby horse,' Craig said. 'Feminist rights.'

'Nevertheless, we'll tell the police . . .'

'I'd rather not,' Nora said.

Roberta Clancy looked at her. 'But you must!'

'Let's leave the subject.' Craig said.

His mother bit her lip. 'Craig's right, of course. I get a bit annoyed at this kind of thing. Unforgiveable of me. But you mustn't go right now, Nora. Stay for supper with us, won't you? Relax and try to put it out of your mind.'

'No, thank you.' Make up your mind and stick to it, Paddy always said. This woman had seemed almost as upset as she had been. Perhaps she was very sensitive. She was a painter. She would be imaginative. 'You're very kind, but I'll get back.' And knowing that was brusque she said, 'You and mother were at school together, weren't you?'

79

'Yes, we were at Ste-Catherine's. I had three brothers and my parents were concerned that I was becoming tomboyish, which they didn't want in an only daughter, especially as I was affianced to a judge's son. Someone told them of Ste-Catherine's and I was sent there to make me into a lady. I'm doubtful if they succeeded, but *your* mother had perfect manners. You went there, too, didn't you? I could tell. Ste-Catherine's young ladies, we were called.'

'Paddy called me Lady Autocrat at times. You know he died?' She tried to stop her voice from trembling.

'Yes, I knew. Laure and I didn't see much – if anything – of each other after we left, but school friendships are lasting. Can you imagine her leaving me this place? I've a feeling it really belongs to you.'

'No, I'm glad. Never more so than now.' She smiled.

'Such a surprise. Laure was quite precocious at school. I think she'd been indulged by her father. Your grandfather, of course. How is he?'

'He's fine. He used to visit a lot when Paddy was alive, but not so much now. He lives near us.'

'Maybe he spoiled her a little. Men can do that with daughters, and Laure's mother had died young. Anyhow, that's past history. She's very happy as Mrs Dexter in Arizona. We keep in touch, birthdays and Christmases, and then that generous gesture of giving me this house . . . I see Craig looking at me. Maybe I gab too much.'

'No, it's interesting to me. You know just as much about my mother as I do. I'm glad she's happy. And it's great that I'll have you and Craig as neighbours. She couldn't have planned it better.' She made to rise. 'But I'll get off now.' She had a great desire to be on her own. It would be easy now.

'Well, if you must. As long as you feel safe.' She walked to the door with Nora. 'I wish I'd been smart enough to notice the number of that car.' They were standing on the veranda.

The late sun was shining, the sky a violet blue. Difficult to believe the terror she'd been in a short time ago. But, oh, the stupidity! It was hard to believe now that the incident had ever happened. 'I feel we should be doing something more for you, like trying to trace this man . . .'

'I could if I wished. I know his name and where he lives, temporarily.' A white lie. 'But I've decided to put it behind me. I'll never see him again. I'm quite sure.' Maybe Richard Trant was regretting his behaviour, too. There had been something good about him, in the cathedral, for instance, and he had been genuinely interested in her house. There were different ways of showing unhappiness. Perhaps he'd had a hard deal, had a grudge against women. *Two sides to every question.*

'Come on, Nora,' Craig Clancy said. 'You look exhausted.'

'Do I?' She turned to his mother. 'Thank you so much. And don't worry. I'm quite good at looking after myself, usually. I'm going to put it down to experience.'

'As long as you're none the worse . . . Yes, you're quite right. Put it behind you. That's what we all have to do in the end. Off you go, then. Craig will see you back.' She embraced Nora warmly. 'Come tomorrow for lunch.'

'I'd like that.' She walked down the steps with Craig, turning back to say, 'Now, don't you worry. I'll be all right.' It seemed to her that she was reassuring Mrs Clancy rather than the other way round.

'I bet you thought Robbie was fussing a bit about telling the police,' her son said as they were walking over the lawn. 'But she's right in a way. He shouldn't get away with it.'

'Away with what?'

'Well, enough to make you shout your head off!'

'*Touché*, she said, 'as they say at Ste-Catherine's.' She laughed. 'Yes, I was scared, yes, it was an unpleasant experience, but he didn't rape me, Craig. I couldn't say that to your mother. I'm quite inexperienced with men, actually.' She laughed to make a joke of it, 'I scare easily.' And that's not the whole truth, she thought. If you hadn't shouted, you *would* have been raped . . . Well, do as you said to his mother, put it down to experience. 'Anyhow, it's a great relief to know you're both there until I go home.'

'Say, don't go away just when we'd got to know you!' He laughed. 'Have you really got to go?'

'Pretty soon, I'm afraid. I'm losing my manager.'

'So you're a business lady?'

'Paddy left the whole thing to me.'

'Oh!' He looked impressed. 'Well, don't make it too soon.'

He came in with her, searched the house, tried the windows, and told her to be sure to close the shutters at night. She had the infamous thought that perhaps she'd become interesting to him because of what had happened.

When they were in the sitting room, he lifted the empty champagne bottle where it was lying and put it on the table.

'A party that got a bit out of hand?' he said.

'That was my weapon. I poured the remainder over him!'

'What a waste!' They laughed. She really liked him.

He wrote their telephone number on a piece of paper and put it on the hall table. 'Don't hesitate,' he said. 'It will save you shouting.'

'Cheeky devil!' She really liked him.

He turned on the doorstep. 'As a matter of interest, what age are you?'

'Twenty-three. What age are you?'

'Twenty-six.'

'I bet you think I'm a dope.'

'I never said a word. Well, I'll leave you in peace.'

She went straight to the kitchen and cooked herself some scrambled eggs and toast because she felt ravenous. But halfway through the meal, she put her head down on the kitchen table and wept. They must have noticed her torn dress. Her own behaviour with Richard Trant had been dubious, tipsily eager to go just a little further, oh, but yes . . . A dope. And then, much later, she wondered what had been the reason for Mrs Clancy's strange reaction when she had spoken of the sitting room, her alarm?

Ten

When Nora got into bed, she found she couldn't sleep. She had thought with all the weeping she had done, she would have dropped off immediately, but instead she had never felt more wide awake.

She castigated herself all over again. There were no tears now. What were you thinking of, asking someone you hardly knew back to your house, playing hot and cold as Richard Trant had put it, where if you shouted until the cows came home, not a soul would have heard you?

Sure, and it was the luck of the gods that Mrs Clancy, Robbie, and her son were there, and that the nice son, Craig, had been sent over to issue an invitation to come for a drink. Someone's been looking after you, that's for sure.

And what would Paddy have said at such stupidity? He who was always warning you about the boyos and their evil intentions.

They aren't all like that, Paddy or no Paddy, and that was the first time she had dared to contradict him in her actions. She could even now put herself in Richard Trant's place. And if they were all the evil devils that Paddy had said they were, how did you explain such a nice fellow as Craig Clancy, or come to that, the person she had known best, Liam? Liam, who had never put a foot wrong with her, nor even a hand . . . and yet the girls were all daft about him. 'Just a star, he is, in them breeches!' Kate

Docherty had said and she wasn't far wrong.

Were all men the same? Liam didn't dare let a hand stray, knowing that Paddy would have beaten him to a pulp, metaphorically speaking, of course, although the truth of the matter was that Paddy couldn't have stood a chance beside Liam's young strength. But, yes, she thought, yes, what was he like set amongst the girls at the county balls? That was the question right enough.

She could imagine Richard Trant's background (and she would put a fiver on it that she was right). City type, married, children, a worry to his wife when he was at home and going out on the prowl when he was away on business. Men like him didn't fundamentally like women, not at all. They had a grudge against them and women wouldn't like him because of this propensity; except his mother, and that would be why she had been visiting him in Paris. Mothers only had white sheep.

Men were deceivers ever, Paddy had said, but that was a sweeping statement. Women could be blamed, too. Richard Trant thought he had scored when he met her, an Irish innocent, but she was to blame as well because of her curiosity. That and the champagne. Now you're thinking straight, Nora.

You asked him to your house, never mind if he suggested it first. And you didn't warn him right away, say, at least, 'Mind, there's to be no funny business, I'm telling you!' But then, Lady Autocrat of Marchmount didn't go around speaking common like that. True, she hadn't had much practice at home. Most boyos watched their step with Paddy around.

The thought struck her as if a sledgehammer had been swung at her. She even winced at the blow, lying there in her bed. Paddy was a youngish man when Laure had walked out on him. Had he become absorbed only in training the finest horses in the land, that and looking after dear little Nora, making sure that Laure was never missed? Or had there been other diversions? Now, there was a thought indeed!

She herself had hardly missed her mother except when she was with other girls and they talked about the things they did with theirs, shopping, chatting, and so on. Apart from that, life with Paddy had been a joy, dressed like a princess, queening it at race meetings as if she wore a label: Paddy Malone's Daughter. Keep off! But what about *Paddy*? He wasn't with her morning, noon and night.

She lay still, her mind full of him, but beginning to understand their relationship. She was fully awake. She knew where she was, in France, in Le Manoir, and that last night Richard Trant had been on the point of raping her when Craig Clancy had battered on the door. Well, it had been a salutory lesson. She must begin to think of herself as grown-up now and put Paddy in his proper place, that of a beloved father who had also his own life.

'Got a bit out of hand?' Craig Clancy had said, lifting the empty champagne bottle and laughing with her when she told him that she had anointed Richard Trant with Veuve Cliquot. 'A new kind of Holy Water,' she should have added, remembering that day when she and Richard Trant had gone into the cathedral and each lit a candle.

Craig had laughed with her. Paddy would have gone mad. She had seen him laying into one of the yard lads and the poor little sod turn into a quivering mass of fear. A hard man, Paddy, except with her. Only Liam really knew him since the time he had trailed after his father. He must have seen how Paddy ran the yard, bullied the managers, lectured the jockeys, insisted on perfection, didn't tolerate mistakes.

Why had she not thought of this before? Or noticed? Because you had to move away to see clearly. There was a before and after. Before Richard Trant and after.

She got up and searched for Liam's letter. She had to tell him. When she found it, she got pen and paper and sat down at the kitchen table. He had said he wasn't staying at Marchmount and she didn't know his address. She looked at the letter again, but the top of it was blank except for the date.

I'm going to give you the shock of your life . . . she wrote.

She stopped to reread Liam's letter: '. . . *never felt it was my life's work* . . .', '*bored with the one topic all the time* . . .' '*When you come home I'll have the accounts ready* . . .' '*I send you my true love, Liam.*'

She sat in the early morning quietness and thought of Liam, who knew far more about running the place than she did, but wanted to leave, wanted a fuller, richer life. Paddy would have gone mad if he'd heard that. She could hear him. 'And will you tell me in God's name where there is a richer, fuller life than training a young thoroughbred? Or training a young daughter until they become part of you?'

But now the spell had been broken. She owned this house in France, a small house with massive ornamental gates which suggested endless possibilities, much exploration, research, all of which appealed to her. And perhaps, when she told her mother what she had found out, she would come and visit. Or Nora might visit her in Phoenix, Arizona.

And there were Robbie and Craig Clancy. And the experience of having almost been raped by an architect – she would never know if that made any difference – and there was Liam. Life had become a rich tapestry, She began to write:

Dear Liam,

I'm writing this letter in the early morning with my thinking as clear as a bell.

Truth to tell, I'm twenty-three years of age, like you,

but not nearly so wise. You know where you're going, and if you don't want to carry on at Marchmount, well, that's good enough for me.

I thought, in my stupidity, that I could take the place over, run it with one hand, so to speak. I might have tried with your assistance, but since you're going, that's not a possibility. Believe me, I'm not trying to persuade you.

When I come home you can show me the accounts and we'll square up and you'll go off to be a land surveyor. I'll put Marchmount up for sale. Your mother will be free to go to the old uncle if she hasn't already done so. It has no appeal for Mhairi without Paddy. I've always known that. She would have done anything for him.

My life is changing. I own a French house near Chartres, an hour in the train from Paris, and now I've met my neighbours, the Clancys, and I've a feeling they're going to become important in my life. I have a different viewpoint, new interests, new friends.

I have so much to hear from Robbie Clancy about my mother and Paddy when they were young, and I shall stay for a week or so to have good cracks with her and get to know them. You'd like Craig Clancy. Also his mother must know a lot about this house as she must have stayed here with my mother when they were both at school in Paris, and I'm hoping to satisfy my curiosity about this small house with its large gates. Remember, I once said I'd like to study medieval history? Well, you may see me at Trinity yet.

I love you too, Liam. I don't know if it's a true love, or a friendly love because we grew up together, but we'll never know until Marchmount is not our background. I realized last night that I hadn't grown up yet, so I'm going to do something about that, and then, who knows? But I can tell you now that next to Paddy, you were always my mainstay.

I'm sending this care of the yard, so I hope it finds you, with my love. Nora.

Eleven

Nora presented herself at the door of the guest cottage full of pleasant anticipation. Craig opened the door to her.

'Come on in. Mother's in the kitchen putting the finishing touches to lunch. We're both dying to see you.'

'Thanks.' She felt immediately shy as she followed him into the sitting room, remembering last night. Before she could sit down, Robbie Clancy came rushing in, holding out both hands to her.

'Welcome, welcome! Well, this is a different girl today, isn't it, Craig?'

'A very pretty one.' He smiled at Nora, and she thought how handsome he looked, brawnier than Liam, and his smile was puckish, almost complicit. 'Would you like a drink?' he asked. 'We have all the French stuff if you prefer it.'

'I do. When in Rome . . . I'd like a Ricard, please.'

'*Avec plaisir.*' His accent was poor, she noticed. The American girls at Ste-Catherine's never managed the French idiom as easily as the British. She had been the only Irish, so she didn't know where she stood.

'Robbie?' Craig asked.

'My usual highball.' She smiled at Nora. 'Come and sit here with me.' She indicated the sofa.

'I'll join you in a Ricard, Nora,' Craig said. He had poured her drink and brought it to her. 'How are you feeling? Did you sleep all right after your . . . ordeal?'

'Thanks.' She took the glass. 'I'd like to say, like a top, but to tell you the truth, I hardly slept a wink.'

'I told you. You should have let me notify the police.' Robbie's face was serious, but not so intense as it had been last night.

'Oh, it wasn't worth that.' Nora sipped her Ricard. 'Honestly. No, I was thinking a lot about Paddy.'

'Were you?' She looked at Nora. 'I suppose that's understandable. You must have been very close to one another. I know how I felt . . . when Bob died. What age were you when Laure left?'

'Ten.' She was sorry she had brought the topic up.

'Was that all? I suppose she wasn't really cut out for family life. But it wasn't as if it hadn't been her own background.' Craig was handing her her drink. 'Thanks, sweetie. He makes a grand highball, this son of mine.' She smiled at Nora, tasting it.

'I believe she didn't like the background, particularly Paddy's: a training set-up, horses . . .' She was immediately sorry she had said that. There was something unpleasant about talking about her mother behind her back. She looked round the room. 'This is nice. I'm so glad she let you have it.'

'Laure was generous to a fault. Shared everything. I'd been before, of course, but when she met Norman Dexter and decided to go back to Phoenix with him, she said I'd be doing her a favour if I would take it over. Lesley and Lois have been with me, but Craig not that often.'

'Oh, why's that?' She looked at him, interested.

'Well, it's a long way and I've been busy at Harvard doing a postgraduate degree. I just finished this year.'

'Oh! That's pretty old to be still at college, isn't it?'

'D'you see my beard?' He stroked his chin, laughing.

'Because I'm a dumb-bell. No, not really. Oceanology's a long haul, but it's great fun.'

'So, now he'll begin to travel all over the world,' his mother said. 'This is his last holiday before he leaves home.'

'So you'll be alone, then?' Nora asked. She was at ease now.

'Oh, I like my own company. Painters need solitude, like writers. Sometimes, if a thing's going well you resent intrusions.'

'I'm good at that, too,' Nora said. 'I don't mean painting, but at being alone. I don't think we'll get in each other's hair.'

'Oh, I didn't mean . . . but you're different. We've so much in common, Laure and I being at school together. I met your father when he came to the race meetings at Chantilly. Laure introduced us. I was engaged, of course.'

'That was young.'

'Oh, it was one of those boy and girl affairs. He wanted me to become engaged before I went to Paris . . . probably afraid he'd lose me.'

'But he didn't.'

'No, he didn't.' She put down her drink and jumped up. 'The lunch is all ready. Why don't we start? Bring your drinks if you haven't finished.' What's the rush? Nora thought.

'The food here is so marvellous!' She led the way into the kitchen, talking all the time. 'The chicken was running about on its two little legs this morning, and the French vegetables, and the fruit! So fresh.'

The meal was in the kitchen, a room as big as the one they'd left, on the opposite side of the narrow hall. Nora guessed there would be two rooms at the back, like her own house.

'Your cottage looks the right size for itself,' she said as she sat down on the chair Craig had pulled out. 'Mine gives the impression of having been knocked up on an impulse.'

'That's about right . . . You carve, will you, Craig. I'll pour the wine.'

'Loire,' he said. 'I hope you like it, Nora.'

'I do. I had some the other day.' She remembered Richard Trant's careful choosing . . . He'd had some good points. What had come over him? Had he been drunk? Or had it really been her fault, giving the wrong signals? 'Do you get French wine in Boston?'

'You can get anything you like in Boston, if you pay for it. Besides there are some educated palates in Cambridge.'

'Bob and I were both born there,' his mother said. 'He died last year.' Her voice broke. 'Here you are, Nora,' she gave her a glass of the rose-coloured wine. 'Perfect for lunch.'

'Thank you. I'm so sorry about your husband. I didn't know.'

'Fifty-two and had a fatal heart attack. It doesn't seem fair, does it, but then, what is?' Craig had put plates at each place with succulent slices of chicken on it. 'Now we're all served.' She raised her glass. 'This is a special occasion. Neither of you know how special it is. Help yourself to vegetables, Nora. It's self-service, here.'

'You were right about the two houses, Nora,' Craig said when they were eating. 'This cottage feels as if it's always been an ancillary. Yours looks, well, rather newer.' And to his mother, 'Did you ever hear about its history, Robbie? Say, from Nora's mother?'

'Not much. It's a long time ago. I always supposed it belonged to her parents. Her mother was French, Parisian.'

'Yes, I knew that,' Nora said. 'I never knew my grand-mother. She'd died when she was quite young.'

'Craig was thinking about going into the library to see what he could find out about Lapantelle, weren't you, Craig?' His mother looked at him and he nodded.

93

'I'd go with you if you do that,' Nora said. 'I'm tremen-
dously interested. Maybe I could write to my mother, or ask
my grandfather, for that matter, when I get back.' She felt
sorry she hadn't seen more of him. And that she'd committed
herself to going home soon, but she had written to Liam. It
was easier for her to come back again. Ireland was much
nearer than USA.

They talked over their lunch for a couple of hours at least.
They told her about Boston and Cambridge and the Charles
River, and she told them about Marchmount and Dublin
Bay. It was about three o'clock when they were drinking
their coffee.

'I don't think we've left ourselves enough time to go to the
library today,' Nora said to Craig, smiling at him.

'There will be other days. This one's too nice to spend
indoors,' Robbie said. 'Why don't you two go for a drive
somewhere while I clear up?'

'Let me help,' Nora offered, thinking she had never done
that with Mhairi.

'Not at all. You go on, and after that I must sort out
sketches and get my gear unpacked and be ready for an
onslaught. I love this area. It suits me down to the ground
compared with Boston which has a salty air. I always feel this
is the heart of France.'

'Or its belly,' Craig said. Then to Nora he added, 'She's
getting the bit between her teeth already. We'd better
clear out. We'll become invisible to her once she gets
going.'

It was a glorious day as they drove through the silent
village on their way to Chartres. 'It's so quiet,' she said to
him.

'Yes, I've noticed. They're not very hospitable, are they,
the French? At home, neighbours would be knocking at the
door and offering slices of pumpkin pie, etc. Actually it suits

Mom. She's still grieving for Dad, and we've encouraged her to go on painting.'

'Is she well-known?' Nora asked.

'She has her stuff in one of the Boston galleries. She doesn't sell much, but she doesn't do it for money. As therapy, it's invaluable. Such a relief to the family. We were beginning to get worried about her.'

'I can understand.' She felt tears spring to her eyes and changed the subject. 'Look at that!' They had reached the main road and the spires of the cathedral had appeared on the horizon. 'Like a beautiful dream, isn't it, shimmering . . . It's worth living in Lapantelle so that you have to drive into Chartres and see that. You won't have been in the cathedral yet?'

'No. I intend to make up for lost time. Perhaps you'll show me around?'

'If I have time. I think I told you last night that I have to go back pretty soon.' She laughed. 'I'm beginning to feel embarrassed at the mere mention of last night. What a fool I made of myself.'

'I'm glad I was around. I don't often see myself in that role – rescuing damsels in distress.'

'Well, it taught me a lesson.'

'I expect you have a boyfriend to go back to?' She felt his sideways glance.

'I don't have a *boy*friend, but I have a friend called Liam who has been running the place for me. Have you a girlfriend?'

'Yes, in a kind of a way. Harry and I have been friends since university days. We're old pals.' Do all the women have men's names, Nora wondered, thinking of Robbie and now Harry.

'Is she a girl or a boy?' she asked. He laughed at her.

'A girl, of course, Harriet. She's always been Harry. We've

95

been on the same projects several times. Great fun. She swims like a fish.'

'Does she?' Paddy had left swimming out of her curriculum, as had Ste-Catherine's. She felt quite annoyed at them both at that moment. 'Does she ride?'

'Horses?'

'Yes.' She stopped herself saying, of course.

'No, nothing like that.' There was a pause. 'Great sight that,' he said, nodding toward the spires.

'Yes, great.'

They drove into Chartres in brilliant sunshine and up to the cathedral so that Craig could see it at close quarters.

'Magnificent,' he said, looking at the Porte Royale, but not too closely. Perhaps they had to be underwater. 'I'll have to come back with my camera.'

'I thought Americans had them perpetually round their necks. Born with them.'

'That's Germans.' He grinned at her. 'You're a cheeky little thing.'

'You didn't think that last night.'

'No, you looked scared to death. Don't you know men yet?'

'Not that kind.'

'What kind is that?'

'Architects.'

He burst out laughing. 'You're pulling my leg.'

'It's the Irish in me.'

'It's certainly coming out.' His look this time was masculine, admiring.

She said, 'I don't think you should go into the cathedral today. You're not in the right frame of mind.'

'Is that essential?'

'Definitely.'

'Well, what would you like to do? When Robbie's painting

she's incommunicado. She won't want to see us till supper time.'

'I tell you what would be nice,' she said. 'Have you heard about Proust?'

'French, is he?'

She burst out laughing. 'Who's pulling whose leg?'

'A bit of both I should think. I did a semester years ago on French writers. I preferred Colette, but never mind. If I'm ever shipwrecked, I'm surely going to have *A la recherche du temps perdu* with me. Even the title's long. Was my accent OK?'

'Not bad for an American.'

'So, why the preamble about Proust?'

'He used to live here with his Tante Leonie in Illiers, not far from here. Would you like to drive there just for the hell of it?'

'For a dignified young lady you have a rough way of talking at times.'

'It's yard talk. You pick it up from the stable boys.'

'I get it. So Illiers it is. I'd really like to follow in the steps of such a great master of the French novel.' They laughed at each other.

'Right you are. I really think you're not ready for the cathedral.' I like him, she thought, as she got back into the car, I really like him.

She soon found out that Craig didn't have what she had – a feeling for history. they located Tante Leonie's house in Rue de Dr Proust which gave Nora an immediate *frisson*, but seemed to leave Craig untouched. She wondered aloud if the street was named after Marcel's father, but noticed he was looking out of the window of the house while she talked. It was the same with the artefacts. Still, I shouldn't blame him for having no feeling for history, she reminded herself, when I have no feeling for science.

She found herself meeting his eyes sometimes, a masculine glance which she had seen often at county balls and against which Paddy had warned her, but she had to admit that it made her aware of her own femininity. Could I fall in love with this man? she asked herself. He would be a masterful lover, but surely she'd had her fill of that with Richard Trant? And hadn't she written at length to Liam only this morning?

They walked about the small town and he put his arm round her protectively, which didn't seem necessary since it was a small town, and told her details of the projects he had gone on, mostly with Harry who seemed ready, willing and able to risk her life on the sea in boats, or under it in a wetsuit. But she cheered herself up by wondering if Harry could control a recalcitrant horse?

'You're a sweet little thing,' he said when they were having a drink at a café – really, they might as well have remained in Chartres. The cafés were better there. 'But you'll have to learn not to be so trusting in future,' he advised her.

'Perhaps I'm risking my life or whatever by being alone with you,' she suggested.

He took that badly. 'That's not my style,' he said, looking away and missing two young Illiers inhabitants who had stopped to embrace each other. She wondered if he and Harry were lovers.

But he was seductive. That puckish grin. There was the delicious feeling of being protected which he gave her, but only if she wanted to be the type of girl who acted as if she needed to be protected. This puzzled her because Harry in her wetsuit hadn't seemed to be that type. Perhaps she was all right for projects where she could take her part, even in bed at the end of the day, but when it came to marriage he needed someone whom he had to protect, and perhaps rule.

There was so much to think about. She now saw that

Paddy had shaped her opinion of the boyos, and she had never thought it out for herself. She could now understand those cool critical looks Liam sometimes gave her. Why hadn't he spoken out? Did he feel she had to discover it for herself?

Denise Pernet could help her there, she thought, so worldly and wise. She made up her mind there and then, while listening to an exciting episode of Craig meeting a shark, that to repay the Clancy kindness she would give a dinner for them in her house before she went back home and invite the two girls and Bettine's boyfriend, Gérard, which would prevent Craig being the only man.

'Marvellous,' she said to Craig. 'I don't know how you managed.' This wasn't a very bright comment, she thought, since he'd spent the last ten minutes telling her how he *had* managed! 'Shall we go now and see Proust's private meadow where he liked to wander for inspiration?'

'Sure,' Craig said. 'Got to get our money's worth, eh?' The tickets he bought had also covered the entry to the meadow.

It was peaceful and beautiful, if you thought of Proust, and at the top there was the half-open gate which was significant, according to the brochure. Even as a child he seemed to have been melancholy and in need of solitude. She showed Craig the postcard she had bought of the significant gate leading to somewhere very private, and although she found that poignant and mysterious, Craig looked at it for a long time and said it was just a gate.

She told him of Proust's cork-lined room in Paris and how she wished she could have sat and listened to all his anecdotes of the *beau monde*. Craig said he'd rather have sat in Colette's bedroom listening to her.

'I have no patience with women who seem to spend most of their time in bed,' she said.

Craig laughed at her, putting his arm round her waist, squeezing it and saying, 'There are worse things!'

They were on good terms on the way home, even to the extent of Craig singing some Beatles lyrics and giving her a passable rendering of *Danny Boy*, saying that Boston was largely Irish, and hadn't she heard of the Kennedys? His voice matched his physique, rich and rumbustious and she could have loved him there and then. She had never been able to sing in cars or for that matter anywhere else. The Clancys seemed to be full of talent.

Robbie was sitting on the veranda when they got back about six o'clock. 'Well, how did you get on?' she asked. 'Craig, a drink for Nora.'

'Definitely not,' she laughed. 'Drink is going to be my undoing if I'm not careful.'

'Especially champagne,' Craig said.

'I'll go home now and touch base, as Craig says. He has taught me some fascinating expressions.'

'Come back for supper, then?' Robbie said. 'You're welcome.'

'No, thank you. But I should like to invite you and Craig to a dinner party in a day or so. I'll have to make some phone calls to the other guests first, if you don't mind.'

'Have you got to know folks in Lapantelle already?' Robbie said.

'No, Chartres. I'd like to return your hospitality.'

'No need, but we'd be delighted, wouldn't we, Craig?'

'Absolutely.'

In her own house she sat down to think over the day. She now had as much company as she liked, and she liked both the Clancys. Life was suddenly full of delightful prospects.

If there was time, she and Craig might go to the library at Chartres and try to find out something more of Lapantelle and their houses. She didn't really need him for that, but she liked his company. He made her feel feminine which hadn't been important to her in the past, but the feeling was new and interesting. Put it all down to experience.

Twelve

Perhaps there's a life without Paddy, Nora thought that evening when she was working in her vegetable plot. It would soon be time to hull up the potatoes and the courgettes had already formed. Loads of water needed for those. Perhaps it was stupid to grow vegetables in this land of plenty, but she was captivated by the experiment. Now she saw why old Aidan clung to his job, nearly bent double as he was. The continual cycle of the seasons and the eternal promise kept him young. And for her, the joy of grubbing in the earth, getting her hands dirty, leaning on her spade and contemplating the result of her labours, planning what there was yet to do, raising her head occasionally to the pleasant view beyond the vegetable plot, all gave her a deep pleasure.

There was a cluster of houses on the horizon which must be the next village to Lapantelle; yet another place to explore, surrounded by the rich golden fields. The belly of France Craig had called it.

Life without Paddy? He had never ruled her and yet she had been dependent on him for love, advice and companionship. The memory came back again of that night when they had sat in the firelight and she had seen his love for her reflected in his eyes.

She could have forged a link with her mother, telephoned, written beyond the occasional letter, but Paddy had been sufficient, and besides, Laure couldn't have wanted them or she wouldn't have gone away. Whose fault was it? All of them, or none of them? She put away her gardening tools and went indoors to prepare for bed.

'Did you hear an owl last night, Mhairi?' she had asked her, and she had said, 'Yes.' Liam had shown her that owl in the barn, hadn't he? A barn owl.

I shall have to tell her of my decision to sell Marchmount, she thought. Her mind had not changed there.

Was there life without Paddy? There had been quite a lot since she left, Chantilly with Richard Trant and then that frightening experience – partly her fault. It did her good to admit it.

Then, meeting the Clancys, liking them and finding in Craig a new kind of man: a handsome American who teased her like a brother, but occasionally glanced at her in a non-brotherly way which made her feel frivolous and flirty and responsive.

How would Bettine and Denise like him? She had telephoned them earlier to invite them to dinner and both had said they would be *enchanté*. Bettine was even more so when Nora had told her to bring Gérard. She had also told them that she had to return home the following week; she had promised Liam. Liam who had always been there and so had lost any mystery.

Was that Paddy's fault? Paddy had liked Liam around because he had trusted him to run Marchmount, but had he adopted a 'dog in the manger' attitude where his daughter was concerned – keeping his little girl to himself. Did Paddy have to die before she could think like this? Had it been necessary to go away, to see that there was a world outside him – and Marchmount?

She had seen his attitude towards her at the race meetings, at the yearling sales, at the county balls, but had not been sufficiently concerned to worry about it. Paddy had always been there, subtly showing her off, another prize possession like the thoroughbreds he trained. But now there was no more Paddy, no more firelit evenings when they talked and laughed together, when he kissed her goodnight.

Richard Trant had demonstrated what men were like when the veneer slipped. It had lain under his sophistication. Was it the same with all of them? Did it lie under Craig Clancy's playfulness, under Paddy's love, although they didn't realize it? Oh, go on, Nora, go on!

In the morning, she called on the Clancys to issue her invitation. Craig had gone shopping for Robbie and she was now waiting for him to come back and give her the car for a painting expedition.

'Stay and see him,' she suggested, but Nora refused. Today was Friday. She wanted to buy food for the dinner tomorrow – she had quite definite ideas of what since she had been an apt cookery pupil of Mhairi's. What she worried about was washing up. Mhairi would have thought it not right to have her perform such a menial task.

She enjoyed her Friday shopping in the busy town and added to it a visit to Denise's boutique where she confirmed her invitation but also bought some small ceramic pots which she would fill with posies and put at each guest's place at the table. She also bought a lacy cloth and napkins to match and at the last moment she discovered some napkin rings to match the pots.

She had seen many different table settings in the hotels where she and Paddy had eaten on their travels. He had been a stickler for an immaculate table when he had guests. He'd maintained it should be an indicator of the food to be served. 'Set their taste buds going,' he would say. As did his choice of the best wines.

She was pleasantly excited when she finished her shopping

and decided to go into the cathedral after she deposited her bags in the car.

The windows in the gloom of the interior were shining jewels of delight, she thought, making her eyes water and she sat in a pew facing the north rose window so she was able to examine it. She knew the squares contained portraits of figures from the Old Testament – they had studied replicas carefully at Ste-Catherine's – and she tried to identify them singly. It took good eyesight, but fortunately she had that.

One by one she concentrated on them and they sprang to life. She found the goodie, Melchizedek, carrying the chalice of faith, and the baddie, King Nebuchadnezzar beneath.

Her eyes were watering again, her glance slewed to Jeroboam and the golden calves, and she thought how sweet and primitive they were. Their colour reminded her of Starlight, the mount Paddy had bought for her. She remembered Liam leading the filly to her, smiling with pleasure and saying, 'She has starlight in her eyes.'

Her thoughts drifted to Liam, to Paddy, to the Clancys, to this new life here and the new life she might have back in Ireland when she sold Marchmount. How would she fare if she had a flat in Dublin and studied history at Trinity? Would she long for Marchmount? Not the bustle and talk in the yard, the horses being led out each morning, but the quiet firelit evenings with Paddy, the dogs lying beside them, his voice in her ears telling her old tales about people he had known.

She wished he was still alive so that she could say to him, 'Robbie Clancy is going to tell me about when the three of you were young and in Paris.' Was it because of those memories that you wanted me to go alone to Chantilly? Did you want me to meet Robbie? It was before she was married, before you and mother were married . . .

Ah, that's enough of the past, she thought, and got up

from the pew. She bought a candle and took it to the alcove where the birthing cloth of Jesus was on show. It was mundane, colourless. You had to look long to realize it was a holy relic. She imagined she heard Paddy's laughing chuckle, and thought, that was one thing we never discussed, our beliefs. Nor their relationship. She had overheard some-one say at his funeral, 'A fine man, Paddy Malone. Beautiful daughter as well. Kept her close at his side, sure enough.'

On the way home she had a sudden idea. She would call on Madame Leroux and ask her if she would mind washing up after the dinner. If she was offended at the suggestion, then she would apologize, but she felt sure they needed the money. Her husband was working in the garden most evenings and making a good job of cutting out beds and digging a path, and seemingly enjoying himself, judging by his smiling face when she pressed an occasional fifty franc note into his hand.

Madame Leroux opened the door, letting the rich smell of garlic escape. She would be busy preparing supper, so she'd better be brief.

'Good evening, Madame Leroux,' Nora said. 'I hope I haven't disturbed you.' As before, she looked flurried.

'He'll be round later, Mademoiselle. Talks about nothing else but your garden. Always wanted to grow flowers, but I told him you don't make money from flowers.'

Nora nodded, tacitly agreeing. 'I'm very glad to have him at any time, but it was you I wanted to speak to, Madame Leroux. I wonder if you would help me with a dinner party I'm giving tomorrow evening. Wait table, wash up?' She tried to look optimistic.

'Tomorrow evening? Well, it just happens I have that free. Sunday it's the Thierys and Tuesday Madame Boez wants me . . .' So there was a rich inner life in Lapantelle all the time?

'Good! Six o'clock, or later?'

'Seven to ten I usually work.'

'Fine, and the usual rate, of course.'

'Eight francs an hour, and I bring cap and apron.'

'Even better. Well, I'll see you tomorrow at seven?'

'*Précisement*. And Monsieur will be with you in half an hour. You're over-paying him, but that's up to you.'

'He's worth every penny.' That remark seemed to win a frosty smile from his spouse.

'*À tout à l'heure*.' She shut the door in Nora's face.

Thirteen

This is one way of turning a house into a home, Nora thought, pleased with her table arrangements. The coarse linen tablecloth had insets of equally coarse lace, the napkins and the napkin rings matched the pottery bowls of pansies at each place, all combining to give the necessary rustic touch.

Her dress matched the tablecloth, not deliberately but because its champagne colour set off her copper hair and her amber necklace reflected the colouring of her hazel eyes. Too much matching, she thought, but she had long ago discovered that white was too stark for her, although Paddy had liked her in it, possibly to emphasize her girlishness amongst the older guests at the Marchmount table.

She had bought the local wines, Sancerre and Vouvray, and a fair sample of local delicacies, crudités, game pâté and, on the fishmonger's advice, a pair of young rabbits, along with the recipe his wife always used, mustard being the essential ingredient. 'Prunes?' he had frowned when Nora had suggested them, 'not in Chartres. Much further south, *le pays sauvage*, but in my opinion even a fresh chicken hasn't the distinctive taste of young rabbit, but, of course, it must be cooked carefully *en casserole*.'

She had decided on an apple tart to follow, with the slices laid in concentric circles and a rich apricot syrup as a final touch, to amalgamate the slices in their pastry flan.

She poured herself a glass of wine and took up her place at the window to await her guests.

Denise, Bettine and Gérard were first to arrive, and immediately filled the cottage with their French chatter. Denise had loosened her hair and it fell about her face in heavy golden waves, making her beautiful and appealing as well as smart. Bettine was in chic black and white, and Gerard echoed this: a formal black suit, white shirt, white aquiline features, a small black moustache, reminding Nora of pictures she had seen of Marcel Proust.

The Clancys must have been looking out for their arrival because they followed soon after. By general agreement, after introductions they filed out again to try out Nora's new garden chairs, where Gérard, having offered to do so, served the wine.

It was a lovely evening, the sky high and with the pale hue of early evening. In spite of the Clancys' apologies for their French, the talk was lively thanks to Bettine's capacity for finishing every sentence which the Clancys started. When Madame Leroux arrived, Nora, excusing herself, retired with her to see to the last-minute details, feeling that, so far, the evening was going quite well.

She showed Madame Leroux the cassserole of rabbit which was simmering in the oven and the vegetables, and was assured by her that she must leave everything in her hands.

'I have brought with me a little bell which you must ring when you have finished each course,' Madame Leroux instructed. She bustled about officiously, patently anxious to have the kitchen to herself.

When Nora went back to the garden, she found Craig and Denise in earnest conversation – at least Denise was talking and Craig seemed to be staring raptly at her face.

'*À table*,' Nora said gaily, concealing her surprise – it

couldn't be chagrin – but decided it was when Craig placed himself firmly at Denise's side at the kitchen table and pulled out the chair which Nora had indicated, saying questioningly to her, 'Here?' and sitting down beside Denise without waiting for a reply.

Nora placed the remaining two women with Gérard between them and took her own seat at the head of the table. '*Servez-vous!*' she said gaily once more and indicated the crudités and the game pâté.

It was a highly successful evening, she kept on assuring herself. The food ably served by Madame Leroux was declared *parfait*, and the talk flowed more freely with each glass of wine.

Robbie and Bettine seemed to get on like a house on fire comparing fashion in their respective countries, and Nora did her best with Gérard. Despite his intellectual appearance, he knew nothing of Proust, nor indeed anything about anything – except *le sport*. He was unable to give her any information about Chartres because: '*Voyez, mademoiselle, Chartres c'est simplement*' – hands turned palm upwards – '*Chartres! Le voici!*' He seemed to imply that it was there when he entered his office and there when he came out again which was all that he expected of it. He had two passions: Bettine and football. No, he knew nothing about *la course*, Chantilly or elsewhere, but he was quite prepared to go anywhere in France to follow his *équipe*.

Madame Leroux had explained that she would serve coffee in the sitting room; it was *de rigeur* in the other Lapantelle houses, but when they went in Robbie remained standing while she looked around nervously, almost as if she had lost her bearings.

'Here's a comfortable chair,' Nora said, puzzled.

'Just look at the sun still shining outside!' she exclaimed in a high bright voice. 'It seems such a pity to be indoors.'

110

The others hesitated, then Bettine filled the gap. 'Shall we all take our coffee outside, then? Gérard and I are stuck in offices all day, *n-est-ce-pas, mon cher?*' He nodded dutifully and they all filed outside, carrying their coffee cups.

It was certainly lovely; the evening air deserving the description of *douce* so often applied to this part of France. Robbie looked happy again and Craig was sitting beside Denise, so all was well. Nora leant back in her own chair, enjoying that pleasant feeling of accomplishment which all hostesses know with the dinner behind them. Mission accomplished, she thought, looking at the high blue sky which was only now turning to violet.

Such a beneficent country, she thought. So much sky, so many acres of golden fields around them, and yet also secret and hidden. Not homely, as the Irish villages were, with cows and sheep in the fields and people visible all the time, eternally talking.

The mystery of the large gates and the small house was perhaps not a mystery at all, Nora pondered. Houses were constantly built on the sites of previous ones. The land might have belonged to her French grandmother, and since she had married Grandfather, an Irishman who already had a mansion, she had need only for a pied-à-terre near Paris.

Robbie was speaking: 'One of the joys of staying here is being able to step outside so easily.' Was she explaining her peculiar reaction when she'd gone into the sitting room? 'Our house in Boston is one of a row of similar houses on Beacon Hill and the gardens are tiny. A town house suited Bob, my husband, when he was alive. He had a law practice in the city.'

'Mother talks of buying a smaller house up the coast,' Craig explained. 'She used to take us to a place called Marblehead when we were small. Great for sailing.'

'I've never been to America,' Nora offered. 'Half of Ireland seems to have emigrated there at some time or other. Paddy, that was my father,' she explained to the French contingent, 'was always travelling about, but never further than Britain.' She added, 'Except Paris.' She had seen Robbie look questioningly at her.

'There's plenty of horse racing in America,' Robbie said. 'Virginia's well-known. Plenty of money in the old southern families there.'

Her son looked up. His attention seemed to be divided between Denise and what was going on.

How handsome he is, Nora thought, and what a fine couple he and Denise would make. There was no point in thinking she had the prerogative on fine young men. The world was full of them. And the other kind. Yes . . .

Madame Leroux appeared amongst them with a satisfied expression. 'Everything is left in order, Mademoiselle. It's ten o'clock.'

'I'll see you out.' Nora got up, excusing herself. At the gates she gave Madame Leroux the envelope which she had put in her pocket, thanked her profusely and hurried back to her guests. 'If you've finished your coffee, do come and see my vegetable plot. It's early yet,' Nora enthused as she led the way.

They trooped after her, seemingly in no immediate hurry to leave. They divided into couples, she and Robbie, Bettine and Gérard, Denise and Craig trailing behind. Well, yes, Nora thought, her hair could knock spots off mine.

The air was warm although it was dusk and far away across the fields the lights of another village twinkled. Utter silence. It was beautiful, but poignant, and Nora recognized that displaced feeling she had experienced occasionally at school: the realization of the essential foreignness of her environment and a longing for home. She said softly to Robbie, 'Do you ever long for Boston when you're here?'

'It's strange you should say that.' She kept her voice low. 'I know exactly what you mean. When I think of Boston I think of my particular area which has an old-world appeal, quite unique, there are even gas lamps in the avenues. But it means my husband to me. Sometimes we would stroll out in the evenings and the lit windows of the other houses, the quiet avenues, gave it quite a Dickensian appeal. Here, you're thrown back on yourself, and, of course, it suits me for painting. Besides, I've memories here of my young days – I said I'd tell you before you go.' Her voice had sunk almost to a whisper as she continued, 'And Craig . . .'

'I'll look in before I leave. Suddenly it's nearly upon me. Would Tuesday suit?'

'Tuesday? Yes, of course . . . no, that's the day Craig and I have to go to Paris. The day after, Wednesday?'

'Fine. I shan't come for a meal, Robbie. I've a lot to pack in as well.' She felt a strange reluctance which she couldn't understand. She was tired. That was it.

'Coffee afterwards. Say about eight-thirty in the evening?'

'Suits me. I'm sorry I'm leaving, it's been so good getting to know you and Craig.'

'Laure will be pleased. I'll write and tell her.'

Perhaps, so shall I, Nora thought.

The party broke up. Denise, Bettine and Gérard were working people, they reminded the others, and it was time to go. They thanked her for what they called a perfect meal, so French. Nora kissed the two girls and said they had nothing to thank her for, it had been a great pleasure to her, and to Gérard she said a special thank you for being her *sommelier*.

'And I hope your team will be successful next Saturday,' she added.

Bettine groaned affectedly. '*L'équipe*! My greatest rival. What shall I do?'

'Go with him,' Denise laughed. 'I've told you that often.'

'But clothes for *le sport*! So unbecoming!' They all joined in the laughter.

They walked to Gérard's car outside the gates, said a quieter farewell because of the quietness of the village, and when the remaining three had reached the foot of the veranda steps, Nora said goodnight to Robbie and Craig.

'A great evening,' he said enthusiastically.

'So we noticed,' his mother said, her eyes going to Nora, her mouth turned up in a smile.

Fourteen

1962

The two girls were in the sitting room at the back of the house at Lapantelle. 'Lovely view from here,' Roberta said. 'Perhaps we should just laze . . .'

'Just laze! We've been incarcerated in that prison for years and this is our first chance of freedom. A day at the races!' Laure looked askance.

'It's so peaceful here . . .'

'We're going to Chantilly. You'll just lo–ve it.' She imitated Robbie's American drawl. 'There will be nothing like that in Boston. Think of the fun!'

'It's all right for you. You grew up amongst horses. I don't know a thing about them.'

'You don't have to. It's a day out, excitement, high fashion, champagne. There's always that around Paddy Malone. And we'll meet some wonderful men!'

'But I'm engaged! What would Bob say?'

'He doesn't have to know, silly. This is a chance to really enjoy ourselves before we leave Paris. I shall miss Paris . . . Never got a proper look at it all the time we were at Ste-Catherine's.'

Robbie's mouth turned down in a sceptical smile. She knew Laure had slipped out a few times – she had been adept at avoiding Madame de Reignier's eagle eye, adept at making

115

excuses, meeting an uncle, or a cousin, when she'd had an assignation. Robbie had envied her, while knowing she hadn't the nerve to do the same.

'All right!' she said, making up her mind. 'It will be something to look back on. Let's get ready!'

'Good for you!'

Half an hour later they stood in front of the mirror in Robbie's bedroom looking at their reflections.

'You're so fair and I'm so dark,' Laure said, consideringly. 'I like your dress. Drifty voile. Suits you. I've gone in for something more *chic*, more striking.' She was wearing a black and white ensemble, and she tilted the large-brimmed hat she was wearing even more, stroked with one arched hand then the other the black gloves which reached to her elbows.

Robbie tilted her pale straw hat which only succeeded in making it fall over her eyes. She laughed. 'At least this way it will hide my blushes.'

'Forget all that. You're no longer a school girl. You're an elegant young lady off for a day at the races. Now, have we got everything, handbags, parasols? Oh, it will be the greatest fun! And Paddy's a charmer, he really is. I know him too well, of course. He'll have no effect on me. We rode together as children, went to the same dancing classes (he dances divinely) and parties . . . Oh, he's a charmer all right, but he knows I can see right through him.'

'That leaves him for me, then,' Robbie said, as they locked up, and stepped delicately in their high heels over the rough lawn and through the massive gates, everything seemed too outsize for the house which wasn't half the size of her own house in Boston. Laure was always fun. Too much fun at times with those bold, flashing eyes. You could be led astray.

'I'm looking forward to meeting the owner's son,' Laure said.

'Which owner?'

'Of the horse Paddy is running for him.' They were now in the car and she let in the clutch. 'He's called Amir and his father's a sheik, can you imagine?'

Robbie thought of the conventional society which was her background in Boston and of Bob Clancy, her fiancé and a judge's son, a practising lawyer himself like her own father. Bob, who had thought it would be advisable for them to get engaged before she went to her finishing school in Paris; sweet, dependable Bob, who wrote lovingly every week, whose parents had bought a house for the two of them already – they'd probably bought his practice, too. What would *they* think if they knew she was going off for a day at the races? They probably thought anything to do with horses as risqué and flash. Not at all the right kind of people to mix with.

Well, they needn't know. She'd worked well and studiously at Ste-Catherine's. She was entitled to have some fun before she married Bob and had babies. He need never know.

The large room behind the grandstand was teeming with people; smart people, well dressed, the women fashionable, the men in morning dress, noisy with laughter and French voices with the occasional surfacing of an American one. Some of the women had long, elegant cigarette holders, but everyone had glasses of what must be champagne. Robbie got the feeling that everyone knew everyone else, that she was in a closed society where wealth and breeding mattered. The Clancys might have been surprised. The people here looked at ease with each other, confident of their position in society.

'Don't be shy! Push in!' Laure was at her elbow. 'I'm looking for Paddy . . . Oh, there he is! Paddy!' she called.

A tall, slim young man in morning dress was making his way towards them. Even a few feet away he gave the impression of handsome, ruddy fairness. There was a dark

117

young man beside him, less tall, but with swarthy good looks, lustrous eyes, white teeth smiling under a small black moustache. Now the tall young man and Laure were kissing, laughing together, chattering.

'Come along, Robbie!' Laure's face was full of laughter. 'This is the famous Paddy Malone! Roberta Durand, Paddy, my school friend.'

'How do you do.' He had her hand in his, eyes smiling, discerning, holding her eyes. His were alive with life and a definite look of appreciation. Did he look at his horses in the same way? 'And this is Amir, my friend, whose father's horse is going to win today. I'm afraid I can't pronounce his second name so you'll just have to call him Amir.'

Amir bowed, smiling. It must be his brown skin which made his teeth seem so white, Robbie thought as she said, 'Amir will suit me very well, then we can be friends, yes?'

'*D'accord*, and all that,' Laure said laughing. 'Oh, and champagne! Thank you Paddy. I knew I could rely on you.' The two girls accepted their glasses, and Laure, sipping, wheeled round to Amir and began to talk animatedly.

Going in for the attack, Robbie thought. All her more outrageous thoughts were never articulated, but Laure was so high-spirited, so audacious, that even the mistresses at school had seemed to be captivated by her.

'So you're at school with Laure, are you?' Paddy was at her elbow.

'Oh, no. We've left now.' He must disabuse himself of the idea that they were school girls. 'We were having a few days' shopping before we went back home for good, and Laure said—'

'That Paddy Malone, her old friend, would like us to come to the races, and you weren't so sure . . . in case you were led astray . . .' Paddy interrupted.

'Oh, no! I was glad to come. It's a new experience for me. I don't mean being led astray . . . racing. I've never been before. My parents—'

'Don't approve of it?' He was laughing at her as he interrupted again.

'No, no . . . just that we have different interests . . .' What were they? she wondered. A round of dutiful parties, galleries, museums, sailing. They had always sailed because of her brothers' interest, and she was considered a good crew. 'We sail quite a lot on holidays.'

'You sail, do you? Isn't that a bit slow, d'you know?'

'Not if you get a stiff wind behind you.'

'Well, you'll have to convince me on that point. This filly of Amir's, his father's rather, goes like the wind for sure. A gorgeous sight indeed.'

'Maybe I should have a bet on it, then?'

'Now, will you let me take care of that for you? Laure will show you the ropes. She was brought up like me, running about in the tack room. Weren't you, my darling?'

Laure turned away from Amir when she heard her name. 'Watch out for this man, Robbie,' she said. 'He's a romancer.'

'A romancer, is it?' He was pretending indignation. 'Now if you're talking about romancers, here's your man!' He put his arm round Amir's shoulders, laughing.

They were both incredibly handsome, Robbie thought, so different from each other. Amir seemed to have eyes only for Laure.

A bell rang loudly and Paddy looked at his watch. 'Time for the Grand Parade. Now that's something that shouldn't be missed for those on their first visit.' His eyes were smilingly on Robbie. 'Come and I'll show you. Hang on to your glass. The champagne comes from a tap here.'

It was impressive and dignified, a kaleidoscope of colour, martial music, applause. It had the formality of French occasions. Robbie sipped from her glass, made polite noises which were drowned by the noise of many voices.

With every sip she lost her shyness and gained in appreciation. Why had she never known about this wonderful world before? She looked at Laure, head back, laughing up at Amir, and found she was doing the same thing, only with Paddy. She found, also, that when their eyes met, he deliberately held hers, as if he wanted her to know something very important. And then, in the midst of all the noise, she heard his voice whispering, 'Where have you been all my life? I've been waiting for you . . .'

She pretended not to hear, then discovered that she was trembling. I'm drinking too much, she thought. I'd better be careful. She applauded when they watched the presentation of the winner's cup, was thrilled when she met the winning jockey and congratulated him, and astounded when she collected her not inconsiderable winnings. And was aware that she was still trembling. With fear? Or with anticipation? She couldn't tell.

Amir and Laure had disappeared. Suddenly they just weren't there. 'Are you going on to the Lafarges?' Paddy said.

She didn't know the Lafarges. 'Is that where Laure and Amir have gone?'

'I don't think so.' His eyes held secrets.

'I don't know the Lafarges.' She was suddenly tired, and a little dizzy. 'I think I'll just go back with Laure now.'

'That would be difficult. At this moment I guess she'll be driving to Amir's apartment. I brought him, so he hasn't a car. Why don't you let me drive you back to Laure's house?'

'But Laure?' She felt childlike, all her pseudo-sophistication, which she had acquired this afternoon, gone.

'Simple. She'll drive herself home – when she's ready.'

'All right.' She made up her mind, managing to smile like a

happy race-goer who had won a considerable sum of money. 'I'd feel safer with you with all my winnings.'

'Safe as houses,' he said, smiling back. He was a charmer. Laure was right. The sweetness of that smile, with the slight twist of the mouth, puckish. *Where have you been all my life? I've been waiting for you* . . . What would Bob say to that?

After they left the Paris traffic behind them, he drove swiftly, once lifting her hand from her lap and kissing it, a sophisticated gesture which nevertheless made her tremble. 'I'm in a dream of delight, d'you know,' he said. 'I knew it was going to be a great day. My dad letting me run this filly of Amir's and then it winning. It had to win to make the day perfect. But even that's nothing compared with meeting you. You're like a . . . princess, or a fairy girl that you'd meet wandering over an Ireland bog who leads you on . . . and on . . .'

'That doesn't sound like me.' She tried to subdue the trembling.

'You don't know yourself. You've been asleep, until now.'

'I hope not, because I'm going back to Boston tomorrow.'

'But you can't do that!' She felt his astonished glance.

'My flight's booked. Everything is arranged.' Including my wedding, she reminded herself.

'Don't tell me any more.'

'All right. I'll not tell you any more.' She felt the slow filling of her eyes with tears, and was able to pretend a cough while she wiped them away. This was a dream, a fairylike dream, bred in Ireland. Bob was a fact, an actuality. There were too many arrangements made, too many promises, commitments, and she wasn't the type to break Bob's heart.

'Why are you crying?' Paddy asked.

'Happiness. And sadness.'

'Ah, well, if that's the way of it, cry away.' When she looked at him his face was impassive.

121

When they got back to the house at Lapantelle she said to him, 'Do you know what, I'm ravenous. A diet of champagne doesn't do much for hunger.'

'There were all kinds of titbits.'

'I know, but I didn't eat any. I was too excited. Do you think I should ring Laure and tell her we're here?'

'No, don't disturb them. Little Laure wouldn't like it.'

'Do you know her that well?'

'Through and through.' Then: 'We both like variety. She's feisty, Laure. At this moment all I can see is a tall, delicate lady in a gossamer dress with dark eyes in a lovely fair face.' He took her hands and pulled her into his arms. Bob had never kissed her like that. He was reserving those kisses for their wedding night. She was trembling, quivering, she didn't know herself.

'I'm going to make scrambled eggs.'

He burst out laughing. 'You do that,' he said, looking at her as if she amazed him, 'and I'll sit in this chair by the window and think of you.' He loosened his tie and took off his morning coat. He unbuttoned the top button of his white shirt. 'This is what we do in Ireland,' he said. 'Do you mind? We're not great men for dressing up in the black and white.'

'No, I like it,' she said. She had assembled the eggs and butter, put the pan on the stove. 'I'm taking off *my* jacket.' She felt her dress deliciously cool with its thin shoulder straps.

'Beautiful,' he said, 'like an Irish wood fairy. I'm the wicked goblin.'

'I hope not,' she said, breaking the eggs into a bowl and stirring them with some milk. He mooched about the kitchen and found Laure's store of wine.

'Scrambled eggs demand a good red.'

She was in some kind of state when he sat down opposite

her. They both played with the scrambled eggs and she avoided his eyes. She felt she might faint.

She said, 'Shouldn't I telephone Laure?' The words sounded strange as if she couldn't articulate properly.

When they were both on the point of putting a forkful of eggs in their mouth their eyes met and his fork clattered on to the plate.

'This is the limit,' he said. 'Do you feel the same as I do?'

'I don't know what that is.'

'Are you afraid of me?'

'I'm afraid of myself. I don't know what's happening to me. It must be the champagne and the wine and wondering if Laure thinks I'm lost.'

'Believe me,' he said, 'the last thing on Laure's mind at the moment is you. Think of yourself for once. Robbie, look at me.'

'I'm looking,' she said, tensing her neck muscles to stop the shivering.

He pushed his plate away from him and stood up. 'Let's be sensible and find somewhere more comfortable.'

'Is that sensible?'

'It's better than this.' He came round the table and helped her to her feet, put his arm round her and led her into the hall. 'What's there?' he said, pointing.

'My bedroom.'

'Couldn't be better. Believe me, Robbie, this is the most sensible thing you've ever done.'

'Laure . . .'

He pretended to strangle her, smiling his puckish smile. 'If you say that name again, I'll . . .' he pushed her gently against the bed so that she fell on it. 'There now.' He lay down beside her.

'Laure . . .' she said laughing.

'What did I tell you? No more, maiden! Now, this is

sensible. We'll lie here and talk sensibly about how we feel, but not for too long, and not too sensibly.' He put his arm under her neck, and her shivering increased. 'Turn round and look at me,' he said.

She did. She laughed again out of nervousness. 'I'm shaking. I don't know what's wrong with me.'

'You've fallen in love. So have I. Darling, I'm going to call you darling. You've never felt like this before. Am I right?'

'Perhaps.'

'I'm different from you. You're so . . . untouched. I swear to God I've never known anyone like you . . .'

She turned to him and said, 'Kiss me.' She thought there was a look of surprise on his face, but he did.

She wondered if at the beginning he had intended to be, well, sensible, hint that he was, well, a man of the world and realized that she was an inexperienced girl, but he was a charmer. And he was a man of the moment. Whether it would have been for ever, well, that she would never know. But it became beyond reasoning. They were swept up in a great tidal wave of feeling. 'Sure and I'll be glad to kiss you,' he said, and his eyes were hot. And then it happened.

Not in a mad rush, but savouring it, as they should have savoured the scrambled eggs which would have been much more sensible. He taught her. He was a talkative man, and he wooed her with words as well as his hands, and she wanted him to go on and on more than anything else in the world. Oh, yes, she knew what she was doing, but it didn't matter a damn.

It was like a day at the races, a kaleidoscope of the unknown until now feelings of excitement. No, more than excitement, of elation, of ecstasy, of all-consuming wanting, until she was satisfied. And afterwards his gentle talking and gentle loving erased her feelings of guilt and of shame, for the time being.

But afterwards, when she was back in Boston, she realized she must have seemed to him like a Christmas present and all he had to do was to unwrap it . . .

It was a long time before Nora got to sleep that night. Robbie's astonishing revelation had shaken her so much that she had left the Clancys early, making the excuse that Craig would want to be alone with his mother.

If *she* had been shaken, Craig had been visibly more so. 'My God!' he had burst out and started pacing about the room, repeating it, then he had stopped in front of Robbie. 'What possessed you! Keeping a secret like that?'

'What good would it have done with both Paddy and Bob alive?' They had both been shouting.

'Calm down,' Nora had said. She had been sorry for Robbie. She had looked terrible, her face a wreck, her eyes sunk in her head. She herself had been forced to ask the question: 'Did Paddy know about Craig?'

Robbie had shaken her head and said that she had married Bob when she was almost three months' pregnant. It had been generally accepted that it was a premature baby, at least she presumed so. She hadn't been able to think straight. Besides, Paddy and Laure had got married after she was back home in Ireland – Robbie had always felt that it was a foregone conclusion.

'Besides,' Robbie had said with a wry twist of her mouth, 'Laure would have torn my eyes out if she'd known. In a queer way she regarded him as her property – after she'd had her fling, and he his.'

Craig had been still unable to believe what he was hearing. 'In the name of God, Robbie,' he'd said. 'What got into you?'

'Leave your mother alone,' Nora had said. Robbie had looked like a trapped animal. 'It wasn't you who was living a lie. Imagine what it was like for your mother.' She had felt

125

she had to speak on Robbie's behalf. She had been weeping hopelessly, helplessly.

Now, lying in bed, she realized that her conception of Paddy had changed. She thought of him at twenty-four in his heyday, attractive, with that puckish smile, full of life and virility, easily smitten, drinking a little too much. His life hadn't just been cosy nights at the hall fire with her.

You could never imagine Liam like that, attractive but not bothered by it, always putting his ambition before his feelings. Mature at twenty-three.

Last night, when Robbie was calmer she had said to them, 'We were good friends, Laure and me, at school. Why, I don't know as we were quite different. I was studious, she avoided work whenever she could. But I admired her for her gaiety and her easy rejection of authority.

'My upbringing had been strict New England, puritanical. Her father, Colonel Maguire, seemed to allow her to do what she liked. She called him the Old Boy. I gathered he'd met his wife, a Parisian, when he was in the Irish Guards. I don't know where they met, but he married her in the early part of the War, I think. Blanche, she was called. She died young. Laure was born in 1943 and she was brought up by nurses and a nanny. Spoiled, I imagine, by her father. Paddy had always been . . . part of her life. They were near neighbours . . .'

I can't think of him any longer as 'my' Paddy, Nora now realized. In his wish that she should go to Chantilly, it had been Robbie he was thinking of. Perhaps, after that episode at Lapantelle, he had tried to get in touch with her, but her mind had been made up. She realized the difference between them. Her future had been planned out for her before she left for Paris, and she was not going to change it.

And how, Nora wondered, would Paddy have felt if he'd

known he had a son? Had Laure kept them apart? These were questions which would never be answered.

An idol with feet of clay, she thought, but it made him human, an ordinary loving father with human frailties. Now she had a half-brother, Craig Clancy, who would always be part of *her* background even if they didn't meet. It would be strange at first. But one thing he had of Paddy's was his puckish smile.

Fifteen

Nora was driving Craig to Chartres the next morning. She had looked in at their house and found him alone. Robbie had got up early, he said, and gone off in the car. She was intending to have a day's painting, she had told him. She felt she had to be alone.

'I can understand that,' Nora said. 'I feel a bit shy of you. Isn't it stupid?'

'Not really.' He smiled at her. 'It was quite a turn-up for the books last night. And here was I thinking of making a pass at you.'

'You don't tell me,' she said, knowing exactly what he meant. 'What about the calf's eyes you were making at Denise on Sunday?'

He laughed. 'I admit it. I'd got to the stage of comparing her with Harry. Difference of night from day.'

'Well, that's your problem. Do you still want to come to Chartres? I'm going to the library.'

'OK. I'm on.'

It was easier to talk in the car. 'But, can you believe it,' she said, 'you and me? Difficult, isn't it?'

'In a way,' he said, 'but, even when I met you first and thought what an Irish charmer you were, there was something there which held me back, a familiarity . . . I don't know how to describe it. Now I know what it was, a kind of . . . family feeling.'

'The first time I saw you I thought your smile reminded me of Paddy.'

'Ah, yes, Paddy.' She knew he glanced at her. 'A deep one, Paddy, even if he was your father. And my mother! The one person you think you know.'

'I wonder if my mother kept the news from Paddy of Robbie's marriage, or if she told him so that he'd see there was no point in him wasting his time? Then, he did what she'd wanted, married her on the rebound. Could it be that Robbie was the love of his life, or he thought so? And that my mother was second best? Suppositions, suppositions.'

'Do you think your mother would guess it had been a rushed marriage?'

'I don't know. All I know is that my parents weren't happy together, otherwise would she have walked out on both of us?'

'Jealousy? Suspicion?'

'How can you tell? I'm pretty sure the young man she went off with was simply a means of escape, as well as a bit of fun. I know it's childish, but I've only recently been able to forgive her for deserting us.'

She had been aware as they talked of the beauty of the spires on the horizon, and she thought again, how constant they were, and how transient we are, all the doubts and suspicions fluctuating in our minds . . . You should get rid of that bitterness, Nora. 'We're nearly there,' she said.

'Nora –' he put his hand over hers on the wheel – 'I want you to know that I'll always be your friend, as well as your half-brother.'

'Thanks.' She was touched. 'I could do with that, sure enough. Well, yes . . . the two of us could make up a little family.' She laughed to hide her emotion. 'That's what we'll be. Then we'll always be there for one another.' The cathedral spires wavered and shimmered ahead of her. She drew one hand over her eyes.

'That's a pact.' He patted her hand.

'Being an only child is no joke at times. You have to work out everything for yourself, and half the time you're treated as a child when you're grown-up and half the time the reverse. Paddy and I were really close, and yet at the end I never really knew him.'

'I was lucky. My father was a friend as well. Very normal, not flash, but you could depend on his word. We were a happy family. The girls spoiled me. I never knew that my mother had any problems.'

'She'd be happy most of the time. You can bury the past if you try hard enough.' She banished the firelit scene at Marchmount, Paddy's eyes on her . . .

'Come off it. You're too young to have a past,' he declared as they pulled up outside the cathedral.

'So you think,' she said, pulling on the handbrake, lifting her bag. 'I'm going in later, but I'll do it on my own. How about the library first?'

'Suits me.'

He put his arm round her shoulders as they walked down to the town centre through the busy streets, and she thought, yes, there's something to be said for having a brother. She was very happy. And there was Liam to go home to. I'm lucky.

The woman at the desk was helpful. There were numerous files on the bombing in 1940 of Chartres and the surrounding villages by the Wehrmacht. Lapantelle was one of them. She gave them some of the files to browse over, and they sat side by side scanning them for about an hour. Chartres, as Craig said, had had a pasting. There was more information than they needed. In Lapantelle, several houses had been destroyed by stray bombs. They photocopied the relevant pages and saw that the water tower figured in one of the photographs. Nora pointed to it and Craig nodded. 'I've noticed it.'

Outside they declared themselves well satisfied.

'Grandfather was always a bit grumpy with me when he came to see Paddy,' she said. 'Maybe he thought I was tarred with the same stick as Laure. I doubt if he ever forgave her for skedaddling. I see now I should have tried harder with him. He must be a mine of information.' And then: 'But I could always ask my mother about Grandma.'

'You could. The distaff side seems to be quite colourful. I'll have to keep an eye on you.'

'Bad stock?' she said, laughing at him. 'No, I've sown my wild oats already, thank you.'

'I know,' he said. 'You could come and visit us in Boston, then go on down to Phoenix and quiz your mother. It would make a wonderful trip, even better, a honeymoon one?' The Paddy smile slanted at her. 'And don't tell me a stunner like you hasn't got someone tucked away in Ireland. This Liam you talk about?'

She slanted her leprechaun smile back. 'I'll keep you informed,' she said, 'but thanks all the same.'

'And in my duties as half-brother, perhaps I should visit *you* and cast a critical eye over this paragon.'

'Do that. And when you come bring Harry . . . or is it Denise?'

'Where exactly is her boutique by the way?' He was casual. 'I thought since I was in the vicinity . . .'

'You'd call in and see her? Well, I'll give you half an hour while I'm in the cathedral and then I'll pick you up there. I haven't a lot of time. Did I tell you I'm off tomorrow?'

'Tomorrow?' He looked surprised and disappointed. 'Not already? Just when I had acquired you.'

'I know, it's sad, but I have things to sort out at home.

Give Denise my love and tell her I'll be back soon. It's nice to think I have somewhere to come back to. We must work out dates to meet in France, then a possible trip to the States, and your trip to Ireland. Yes, you must come and see March-mount before I sell it. Suddenly my life seems very full. It's all developed since I came here, especially with meeting you and your mother.'

'And there was your architect friend.' His smile was wicked.

'Don't make me blush, you devil.'

He kissed her when she left him to go into the cathedral.

She felt at peace when she sat in her usual pew. How good it was to have a place like this, always ready to receive you. The jewelled windows were more beautiful than ever, the gloom was a velvet gloom. She sat quietly, lulled by the peace. She watched people walking around, some standing still while they raised their heads to the windows as if for a benediction. It was there for the asking.

She lit two candles, one for Paddy, dead, and one for Craig, alive. Liam was different. Paddy and Craig were family, Liam – well, she still had to decide about him.

Sixteen

R obbie and Craig saw Nora off at Chartres Station. They
had wanted to accompany her to Paris and the airport,
but she'd disagreed. She hated prolonging farewells.

'To find you and then to lose you so quickly is heart
breaking,' Robbie said tearfully.

'But you aren't losing me,' Nora said comfortingly. 'Think
of the gain for me. A family.'

'Yes, cheer up,' Craig said. 'It's a new beginning. We're all
looking forward to many happy visits here and in America
and Ireland. Life's going to be a whirlwind of pleasure. The
only problem is, I have to work for a living.'

'So have I,' Nora said. 'I think . . .' She still had her dream
about Trinity. She was finding in herself new modes of
thought which were probably inherited.

She climbed into her compartment. The train started. She
waved enthusiastically and then sat down. When it's over, let
it go. France had been a wonderful experience, a lot had
happened, but now there was another life ahead of her.
Perhaps this attitude came from her mother. She had been
pretty good at cutting loose when it suited her.

In the train, whizzing along to Paris through the *douce*
countryside – Maintenon, she saw the notice – she thought of
her mother. Had she felt second best with Paddy all the time,
or had it nothing to do with his short-lived affair with
Robbie? Simply that he had turned out to be a philanderer,

and not a very careful one at that. She was amazed that for the first time she was on her mother's side. Had she put off her mother by being so obviously Paddy's property?

But again she thought, even if I asked mother, I'd only get one side of it. Let it go. It was the future which mattered, Marchmount, Liam, her own career when she sold Marchmount. History. Medieval history. Chartres cathedral had given her so much pleasure, not only from the point of view of religion. So much to think about. Amazing how she had shelved it all when she was in France, since Chantilly. Now the day of reckoning was fast approaching.

In the taxi taking her to Charles de Gaulle airport (as an heiress she was entitled to hire a taxi instead of going by train or bus), she thought, this is the hiatus between my two lives, between two countries. It had all started from that wonderful day at Chantilly. She remembered the two happy young couples and the Trants. And Richard, so polite when Mother was around, so unhappy on his own that he had to go about despoiling or trying to despoil young women in order to forget his own unhappiness. Good luck to you, she thought, although you don't deserve it, treating me like scum, and then she remembered her own eagerness and felt ashamed. It was a different girl indeed going back to Marchmount and Liam . . .

He was waiting for her at Dublin airport and oh, the elegance of him in his dark suit and striped club tie! The darkness of the suit made his hair glow like golden silk and she thought, It's wasted on a man, but then remembered that he liked hers. Copper nob he had called her when she was young. She went into his arms naturally but it was more a welcome home embrace than one of passion.

'I thought it was a shame you arriving here on your own,' he said. 'I got your letter.'

'It was good of you to meet me. I didn't expect it.'

'Well, it's all the more welcome then,' he said. 'Come on.' He lifted her luggage and loaded it on to the trolley he had acquired. She followed him to his shabby station wagon. It didn't match his suit.

'Why are you dressed up like that?' she asked when he was driving out of the airport.

'The suit? Bought it for the race meetings. The owners like you to be there and the jockeys are always looking for last minute tips. Besides, I couldn't let Paddy down. Remember what a toff he always was? He loved it.'

'And you don't?'

'I like a bet as much as the next one, but the responsibility of training a thoroughbred? No, but no. It's worse than being a first-time father.'

A fat lot you know about it, she thought.

'I haven't accepted any new ones, as you said you would be selling up. I'm not good enough, and anyhow it's too time-consuming. *You* could spare the time, but you haven't my knowledge and skill.'

'Thank you very much. So all the times I went to race meetings with Paddy didn't mean anything to me at all?'

'Oh, you liked the occasion, but you lacked Paddy's flair.'

'And what was that?' Some homecoming, she thought.

'Spotting a winner in a young horse brought to the yard for training. Paddy's judgement was unerring.'

She hated to be cut down to size and retaliated with a complaint: 'You might at least have waited till I saw if I needed you longer?' She took a glance at the elegance of his shoulders in the dark suit, the pleasing shape of the back of his head. He left them all standing, she thought, feeling more annoyed with him than ever. 'I have to get busy and sell Marchmount and then there's my idea of going to Trinity.'

'Have you applied?'

'No, but I'll get in. No trouble.'

'Paddy spoiled you,' he said. 'I had to work like the devil for years . . .'

'But you weren't as well educated as I was.'

He shot her an amused look. 'Still the same nose-in-the-air Nora. But beautiful with it.'

'Don't soft-soap me.' She hid a smile.

'Apropos Marchmount, there are quite a few people interested if you're serious about getting rid of it.'

'What else can I do? You won't stay on, and since I'm not capable of running it, according to you, and I'd have to get a really good trainer to keep up its reputation . . .'

'I really can't, Nora. I'm committed. I had an interview with my new employers this morning. They would like me to go abroad pretty soon. That's why I'm in this stupid mufti.'

So it hadn't been for her. Hard cheese, Nora. She looked at him again. Leaner, a little older, but that was silly, she had only been gone a month.

'I feel you looking at me,' he said. 'The bags under my eyes are with running your place and travelling to Dublin every day. Did I tell you I'm bowled over by your beauty?' She gave him a good push on the shoulder. 'That's Nora Malone all right,' he said. 'Home to torture me again. The smart young woman I met at the airport didn't look like her at all.'

'That was my *je ne sais quoi* look . . .' She was defeated. 'I had a marvellous time, Liam.'

'I had a hell of a time. People bothering me to know when you'd be back, and horses, horses, horses when I'd rather be a land surveyor.'

'You were being paid by me.'

'I didn't draw any money. I did it for love.' His voice was matter-of-fact.

'Well, that's one saving.' She wasn't going to go down on her knees. 'Is your mother still there?'

'On and off. She's keeping your place tidy, but she has to be with the ould uncle morning and night, to get him up and put him back to bed.'

'Have you been staying at Marchmount?'

'No, it's yours.' He'd always been against that. She would stop squabbling with him. It was partly tiredness, but at the same time he could be bloody annoying. Race track talk, Paddy. There would be no Paddy to welcome her, never, no more. She wallowed in sentimentality, feeling the tears swilling about her eyes.

'I love Dublin,' she said, thinking what an uncharacteristic, sugary-sweet remark. 'Would you drive through instead of taking the bypass? Do, please . . .' She clutched his arm dramatically and he shook it free.

'Cut it out. I'd like to but I've got to get us back quickly. There are still the horses to see to. Diets. And the vet's coming. Crackers has a bone coming through. What a damn silly name! Mother has left a meal for you. She'll be round to see you tomorrow.'

'That's fine.' She always used to be on the steps to greet them when she and Paddy came back from one of their jaunts. Yes, it would be a shell without him. Time to go.

'Her life hasn't been a bed of roses. The ould uncle' – this seemed to be the title he'd given him – 'and before that, my father being killed. But she said she'd never forget the fine time she had with you and Paddy at Marchmount as long as she lived. She was sorry it was all over.'

'Did she say that?'

'Yes, she did. "Them were grand days, Liam, my boyo," she said, wiping away a tear.'

That was a bit snide, she thought, but when she glanced at him there was sadness in his face in spite of the joking.

'Would you come up to the house and help me to eat what your mother's left? I know her idea of "leaving something".

Besides, I've something to tell you.' She knew he looked at her quickly.

'You haven't gone and got yourself married in France?'

'No, nothing like that. Eight o'clock?'

'Make it eight thirty.' He grabbed her when she was getting out of the wagon and kissed her hard. You never knew where you were with Liam.

Seventeen

Liam arrived at eight thirty in his breeches and sweater, smelling slightly of horse dung.

'I've been bedding them down,' he said. 'Do I stink?'

'Just a *soupçon*.' She wrinkled her nose. 'We're full of showers here.'

'Thanks, but unless I could change, it would still be there. Sorry. You'll have to put up with it. What did my mother leave?'

'Soup and then a casserole. It's in the oven hotting up. That's about it. Fruit.'

'Knowing her casseroles, it will blot out everything else. I've brought a bottle of Medoc.'

'Thanks. There's always plenty here, but all right. You open it while I'm dishing up.'

Mhairi was a good cook. The soup was proper soup, her favourite consommé made with 'real beef', she always reiterated when there was anyone to listen to her and, as Liam said, it made a hell of a difference.

He told her that the manager who'd been temporary had left, but the stable boys were good, and Sammy, the oldest one, had a head on him and listened to what he was told.

'Marchmount is finished temporarily as a training establishment,' he said, pouring the wine. 'I haven't accepted any new horses because I don't want to spoil Paddy's reputation,

139

but two of the men wanting to buy would carry on with the yard tenanted as it is. The owners of horses already here are agreeable to this arrangement provided there isn't a gap, but you would have to move fast. It's peak racing time just now.'

'I know.'

'The price is right.'

'I know. I read your report.'

'Will you miss it?' The grey eyes were on her. She had never been able to lie to him.

'It's just a shell now. I couldn't live here without Paddy.' His eyes still held hers. He sipped his wine, waiting. 'Yes, I'll miss it, but I've given you your answer.'

'Good. Knowing when it's time to go is difficult. I had the same problem when I decided to give it up. I've trotted after my dad with a bucket from the time I was three.'

'You probably saw me doing the same thing.'

'I can remember you distinctly from then.' His eyes grew fuller, warm.

They reminded her of Paddy's eyes as she said, 'Liam. Do you still have owls in the barn?'

'What made you ask that?'

'Just a memory.'

'Yes, they're pretty constant. They breed several times a year. I still see them when I'm late at the yard locking up.'

'But never near the house?'

'What's this? No, never near the house. Only in the barn. That's why they're called barn owls. *Comprenez-vous*, Frenchie?'

'*N'importe*. And you couldn't hear their shriek here?'

'It's too far. And you're surrounded by trees. Have you gone mad?'

'Just my old delightfully crazy self. Are you going to scrape the pattern off that Worcester?'

'A man's got to eat.' He grinned at her and she thought,

140

Even if he's far too good-looking he's still attractive. Very.

When they were sitting at the fire with their drinks, she said, 'Prepare for a shock.' She saw the alarm in his eyes and thought, it isn't fair.

'Something happened in France.' The alarm increased. She saw a muscle move at the side of his mouth.

'Go on.' He was stern, unsmiling.

'I discovered I had a half-brother.' The relief on his face was instantaneous.

'A half-brother! It's a hell of a shock, certainly, for you. Me too. I thought you were going to tell me that you'd got married.'

'It's not so easy, in France. Quick marriages. He's my mother's friend's son. And Paddy's.'

He drew a deep breath, and was silent for quite a time. Then: 'How did you find out?'

'Mother had left the guest cottage to this friend, Robbie, she's called, and her son was there too. Craig. Twenty-six. I fancied him at first. It bowled me over, but, well, I have a family now.'

'Yes, that's good. Only children are sometimes lonely. I've felt it. One way to change it is to marry and have children of your own.'

'Do you intend to?'

'Yes, lots.'

'There speaks the selfish male.' She smiled at him and for once he looked vulnerable, almost as if he'd meant it. 'Well, that's my piece of news. I've got a half-brother now. I've made two good friends, and I think they'll visit me here . . .' She looked at him suddenly, her hand to her mouth. 'But I won't be here.' A small moan escaped. They were sitting side by side on the sofa in front of the fire and he put his arm round her shoulders.

'It's sad. Sad for me, too.' She remembered that she had

141

sat on a sofa with Richard Trant not so long ago and wondered if she should tell him that as well. Tears welled up in her eyes at the thought of leaving Marchmount and the mistake she'd nearly made with Richard Trant.

'Don't cry,' he said, 'or you'll start me off. Would you like more wine?'

'No, that was my undoing.'

'What?' The alarm had sprung into his eyes again.

'I mean. That could be my undoing.'

'And mine.' He kissed her cheek, then jumped to his feet. 'I'd better be going. I'm back at the yard at five before I go to work in Dublin. Thanks for my meal. It was good.'

'Thank your mother.' Her tears had dried. Let it go, Nora, let it go. 'Would you arrange for me to see the buyers as soon as you can?'

'Sure. Get some sleep. You're washed-out looking.'

'I was as beautiful as ever not so long ago.'

'Beauties can still be washed out.' He looked down at her. 'Do you know what I'm seeing just now?'

'A beautiful washed-out beauty?'

'No, a little girl of three with red plaits, carrying a bucket.'

They looked at each other, and she thought, This is a dangerous moment. His eyes were very warm, verging to hot. The muscle was moving at the side of his mouth.

'Copper, if you please. Paddy said like beech leaves.'

'Ah, well, Paddy was a man for the words.' She thought she must look quite inviting, but he didn't try to kiss her.

In bed that night she thought how once, a long time ago, Liam had taken her into the barn to see the owl.

'Oh, he's looking right at me!' she'd said, covering her eyes from its unblinking round black gaze, the curved autocratic beak. It had been its absolute immobility which had scared her.

'Don't be afraid,' he'd said. 'Look at those soft creamy-

142

coloured wings. It's a young male. Only the chicks are snowy white.'

Still immobile, it had suddenly let out a loud piercing shriek and she had turned her face against him, terrified.

Liam was right. They were too far from the barn to hear it here, but Mhairi had agreed with her. 'Shrieking like a banshee,' she'd said. She'd been a liar, and she, Nora, had been the simpleton.

Let it go, she said, just as you've almost succeeded with Richard Trant. Think of the future instead.

Liam telephoned her in the morning and said he had made arrangements for the two prospective buyers to call, one at ten a.m. and one at eleven a.m. He was sorry he couldn't be there as he would be at work, but in any case, it was her decision.

Well, yes, she thought, but I could do with some moral support.

The first man was young, well-dressed in expensive hacking jacket and jodhpurs, shiny boots, as if he'd been rigged out for the interview. Money was no object, he said that his father would foot the bill. He was more interested in Nora than Marchmount at first, but she soon put a stop to that with a few of her haughty airs.

Daddy had bought a young thoroughbred which he'd like to be properly trained, and they were both keen on racing. From the other side of the rails, she thought.

She promised to let him know tomorrow. She apologized for not showing him round herself, but she had another client to see. He didn't look over-pleased when she passed him on to Sammy, who in his late years had grown more like a leprechaun than a stable boy, with his large torso and short legs which were due to spending most of his time on the back of a horse.

The second buyer was in fact twin brothers from Roscommon who already owned a yard but wanted to be nearer Dublin and the airport. They had been lucky with horses at the English meetings. Cheltenham, she wondered, remembering Grace Trant.

They'd seen round the place. It was in good order and big enough for their needs. They liked it and would offer her five thousand less than the asking price for a quick sale and a promise that they would restore Marchmount to its former glory.

'A lovely man, Paddy Malone,' they said. 'We wouldn't let him down.' She told them she'd had a better offer, but she wouldn't overlook theirs when she came to a decision.

'And have you no one at your elbow, now?' one of the brothers said. 'It's a big decision for a young woman to be making.' He hadn't heard of feminine emancipation.

'Oh, I'm used to making big decisions,' she told him, but his brother gave him an impatient look and said they were damned if they would increase their offer. She had earlier made the mistake of saying to them that the welfare of Marchmount and its continued success was more important to her than money.

After they'd gone, she thought of having a walk round the old place, but she knew it would only break her heart: the yard, the bustle, the white fence where she had so often leant watching the horses going through their paces. And that green, soft landscape melting into the hills. Even the usual smell might add to her misery, she was prepared to admit. No, it was time to go. It was the actual going that was the hard bit.

She was sitting in the recess of the drawing room window, trying not to feel too dejected when Mhairi arrived. She didn't know whether to treat her as an enemy or a friend, but reminded herself that she had let it go. Paddy had loved her and she had loved him ever since Laure had walked out and

144

left them. What he had done with his life when she wasn't with him had been his own business.

Mhairi looked paler and thinner. 'Well, Nora,' she said, 'back from your travels, is it?'

'That's what it is. How are you, Mhairi?'

'Worn down by the ould uncle. It's a penance, sure enough, but never mind, I had a fine time when I was here.'

I bet you had, Nora thought. What a dolt I was, but, no, let it go. Paddy had been a man of many loves and he'd left her a better memory than a dream, a living, breathing half-brother.

'I met my half-brother in France,' she said. 'The son of my mother's friend . . . and Paddy.'

Mhairi's mouth dropped open. 'Am I hearing right? Paddy's son!' She fell into a chair. 'Are you telling me that Paddy had a son . . . what age was he?'

'Twenty-six.'

'So he was born about 1963?' She was good at arithmetic.

'That would be about right.'

'Let me see . . . that was around the time my Seumus won the Prix de Diane (she called it 'Pricks'), at Chantilly?'

'Yes, that's right. What age would Paddy be?'

'Twenty-four. Ages with my Seumus.' Had she ever said, 'my Paddy?'

'You knew he asked me to go to Chantilly again?'

'No, I didn't. But he was sentimental, Paddy . . .' She looked into the distance.

'The mother of my half-brother is called Robbie – I don't know what her maiden name would be then, but she is now the widow of a Mr Clancy.'

'Was she American?' Her eyes lit up with comprehension.

'Yes. She is.'

'I remember my Seumus saying that there was an American girl along with Miss Laure to see the racing. They'd both

145

be nineteen, just left school. A half-brother!' Mhairi still looked as if she had received a body blow.

'His name is Craig.'

'Craig?' It didn't seem to help. She sat in silence for quite a time and then jumped to her feet. 'I'll go and make us a cup of tea.'

'That would be nice, Mhairi.' Nora thought she saw the beginnings of a smile round the woman's mouth.

Mhairi stopped at the door. 'Colonel Maguire is not so well these days. A slight stroke. That's another one who's missing Paddy.'

'I'm sorry to hear that.'

Eighteen

The next day the telephone rang quite early. The woman speaking sounded slightly American to Nora. 'Robbie!' she exclaimed. 'Where are you phoning from? Are you still at Lapantelle?'

'It's not Robbie.' Nora was speechless. She waited. 'It's Laure. Your mother.' Of course it hadn't been Robbie, the voice had been deeper and with only a slight American inflection. She sat down suddenly, shaking.

'Nora?' the voice said.

'Yes, I'm here. You mean, you're my mother?'

'Yes, your very own wicked mother.' She imagined a hidden smile. 'You're not going to hang up on me, are you?'

'Oh, no. It's just such a shock. Where are you?'

'With my father, your grandfather, at Lisborough. He's been poorly.'

'Yes, Mhairi told me last night. I've been away, you see. I'm sorry about Grandfather.' She always thought of him as a remote figure who remembered her birthdays and Christmas generously, but had been more interested in Paddy. He had told her that Eddie (she never thought of her grandfather as having a first name) felt guilty in Nora's presence because of his daughter's behaviour. This recalcitrant daughter was now speaking to her in a quick, brisk fashion.

'Could you jump into your car and drive over? We can't talk on the phone?'

147

'Yes, I can.'

'Right away?'

'Right away?'

'I'll be waiting for you.'

'Ok.' She tried to think of a suitable parting remark, but couldn't. 'Ok,' she repeated.

Despite her promise to hurry, she took a little time to doll herself up. She had to get used to the idea of her mother a few miles away from her. She chose a silk shirt, a pale beige skirt (trousers were her norm) and good shoes. She brushed her copper hair thoroughly, even sprayed some French perfume over it, then carefully applied a coral lipstick. She noticed her hand was shaking.

I'm ready, she said to herself in the mirror. If she had been going to meet a man she couldn't have been more particular, but her mother! Bejasus! She tried to steady herself.

Laure was at the door when Nora got out of her car. At the last minute she had picked a bunch of flowers from the perennial border – Aidan would kill her. He had a special patch for house flowers in the vegetable garden, but never mind. Pink peonies, white phlox and yellow daisies, some blue delphiniums – a discordant collection. Now she grabbed the bunch from the back seat and running up the steps towards her mother, she held them out with a smile but feeling terribly embarrassed.

'For you,' she said. Her mother's embrace crushed the flowers between them and half of them scattered at their feet.

'Oh, I'm sorry,' Laure said. Nora saw that she was crying.

'Never mind.' She scooped them up and added them to the ones her mother was holding. 'There, now.'

'Oh, Nora!' She mopped with a handkerchief. 'I don't know what I'm doing. Come in. Daddy's in bed. We can go up later.'

They were in the large hall which Nora remembered from a

Christmas dinner a few years ago. It was bigger than the one at Marchmount, more comfortable with its carpeted floor and it was flooded with light from the round window in the roof. Marchmount was dark in comparison, but cosier in winter.

Laure put the flowers down on a side table and called loudly, 'Cecilia! Will you be putting the flowers my daughter has brought me in a vase!'

She didn't have to go overboard with the Irish accent, Nora thought, then thought of Cecilia whom Paddy had once called bog Irish. But then hadn't Laure called Kevin Flannagan, the young lover she'd gone away with, the same?

'I'll be doing that in a minute, Miss Laure.' There was a distant cracked voice. She must be about a hundred and ten now. 'As soon as I finish making this coffee you wanted for you and your daughter. Coffee, she said, it had to be coffee. Tea wasn't good enough, oh dear, no.'

Laure tossed her head upwards at this droning monologue, clicking her tongue. 'Do you remember the old battle-axe?' she said. 'She won't be hurried.'

Could you ever forget her, Nora thought, following her mother into the drawing room. 'Yes, I remember Cecilia. She's always been here.'

'She came when I was five as a nanny. She'd have been twenty-eight at the time, a disappointed spinster, so that makes her about seventy now.'

When they were seated her mother said, her eyes red with rubbing them, 'Now we can look at each other, say what we really think, and then I'll grovel. You've no idea how ashamed I feel.'

'There's no need to grovel,' Nora said, slightly Ste-Catherine'ish. 'You look quite different from what I remembered, all the same.'

'Tell me what you remember?'

'You had rosy cheeks and black eyes and tumbling hair the same colour and you could be very jolly, but you often hadn't time for me. Especially if Kevin was hanging around.'

'Oh, don't mention him! Bog Irish! What am I like now?'

'Your rosy cheeks have gone.' The difference between a rosy apple and an orange, slightly dried-up.

'That's the hot, dry air out West. It's not good for the skin.'

'And you've gone blonde?' It didn't suit her at all.

'Dyed. It was going grey at an alarming rate – very black hair always goes sooner, and so this is what my hairdresser calls a sensible solution. There are more blondes in Arizona than in the whole of Scandinavia. But you . . . it isn't fair! Why mothers leave home—'

The door was suddenly kicked open by Cecilia bearing a large tray loaded with a large coffee pot, cream jug, sugar basin and plates of sandwiches. She staggered in, then plonked it down on a table, tucking a wisp of grey hair behind one ear. No sensible solutions for her.

'I thought you two would be having a good crack so I made a pile of sandwiches to keep you going: river salmon and egg and cress.' She looked accusingly at Nora. 'Well, miss, you're a stranger here, I must say. You used to come with your father, God rest his soul.'

'That was when I was younger, Cecilia. Then I went away to school. Paris.'

'Like the rest of them,' she said, nodding, her mouth turned down. 'What do you think of your mother coming back here as bold as brass, eh?'

'I'm very pleased to see her,' Nora said carefully.

Laure looked haughtily at Cecilia. 'I gave you a good reason, remember?' Her voice was steely. 'I wrote. Mr Dexter has been ill for some time.'

'Your fancy man?' retorted Cecilia.

150

'Watch your tongue. I'm Mrs Norman Dexter now.'

'Better late than never,' Cecilia said, then to Nora, 'And as for you, you're finished with school now so I'm sure the Colonel will be glad of a visit, confined to bed as he is half the time, poor soul.'

'If you don't stop bleathering,' Laure said, 'the coffee will be cold and these sandwiches stale. And take the flowers with you.'

Cecilia gave them a scornful look as she swept them up. 'They're not a patch on what we have here. Ould Aidan's past it.' She looked round the room, nodded slowly, once or twice, and went, deliberately slowly, giving every impression of having been kicked out.

'Miserable old bugger,' Laure said. 'She still talks to me as if I were learning to ride my first pony.' Nora laughed and changed the subject.

'What's wrong with your husband?' Should she have said, my step-father?

'Parkinson's. He's on the best treatment we can find. He'll travel anywhere to get it, so it keeps us busy. It was he all the same who insisted I should come home and see Daddy when I found out he was ill. He's a truly good man, Nora. Goodness lasts longest. I've learned the hard way.'

'I didn't know you were married?'

'Yes, when Paddy died. He wouldn't divorce me, you know. Ah, well . . .' Her face softened, smoothing out the wrinkles round her mouth and eyes which she said had been caused by the hot sun.

'Why didn't you come to Paddy's funeral?' She spoke to Laure's back. She was pouring out the coffee.

She turned and handed her a filled cup. 'He never forgave me for running off.'

Nora was tempted to say, Nor did I, but would have to have added, at the time.

'Help yourself to cream and sugar, and take a sandwich,' Laure said. The subject was closed.

'Thanks. What's wrong with Grandfather?'

'The doctor thinks he's had a slight stroke. Cecilia's exaggerating as usual. Doctor Ryan wrote to me. It's mostly loneliness and a bit of self-pity.' Nora felt guilty. 'Norman said I'd regret it if I didn't come and see him in case he popped off. I've got enough in my life to regret.' She sat down with her coffee. 'Have you forgiven me?'

'Oh, Mother, it's long ago!' She was feeling love rising up in her. 'I hated you when I was ten, but Paddy soon filled your space.'

'Putting the boot in? Ah, yes, you were always Paddy's girl. You had no time for me.'

'I have now. I'm selling Marchmount and I need some advice.'

'Selling Marchmount!' She put down her cup. 'In God's name! Whatever for?'

'I won't have time to run it, because I intend to go to college. Marchmount is full of memories of Paddy. I want to shake myself free of him.'

'You'll take him with you wherever you go if that's the case. I did. Maybe you should put someone in his place. Help yourself to another sandwich.'

'No, thanks.'

'Well, this is a surprise, but don't think I grudge him leaving it to you. I don't need it. Do you mind me smoking?' She had lifted a cigarette case and a long ebony holder from the table beside her.

'No.' It dries up your skin.

'In any case, Lisborough comes to me,' she said, 'and I've got many happy memories here. Not many of Marchmount, truth to tell.' She blew out smoke. 'And money isn't important. Norman has taught me that and he's got plenty of it. Only health. More coffee?'

'No, thanks.' They hadn't struck the right note yet. They should have been reminiscing, but she had left when Nora was too young and all her happy memories were of Paddy.

'You haven't changed, you know,' Laure said. 'Just taller, but still with that devil in your eyes when you're being as sweet as honey.'

'Paddy said I had a leprechaun smile.'

'Paddy was a man for the words.' Liam had said the same thing. She thought her mother looked pitiful here, though smart, with her orange skin and her blonde hair.

'I'd better tell you about the two prospective buyers,' she said. 'One will pay the price asked. His father has plenty of money but they haven't any experience, the others, two brothers, have plenty of that but they want it for five thousand less than the asking price.'

'Money is no object, it's what's best for Marchmount. I tell you what, we'll ask my father when we go up to see him.'

'That would be an idea. I haven't visited him much, I'm sorry to say . . .'

'I'm guilty of that sin of omission, too.' She looked at Nora. 'When you thought I was Robbie, does that mean you've seen her recently?'

'Yes, she was in the guest cottage at Le Manoir. I'm just back from Lapantelle.'

'I wanted you two to get together. A bit of a wheeze.'

'Oh.' Food for thought. 'Perhaps I didn't express myself very well when I thanked you, but now that I've stayed at Le Manoir, I've a . . . family feeling for it. Especially because of Robbie . . .'

'Did she spill the beans?'

'Yes, she did. Craig was there. Her son.'

'And Paddy's.'

'Did you know?'

'I've always suspected it. She was in a terrible state before she went back to America, weeping and wailing. I knew something had happened.'

'I was bowled over. So was Craig. He didn't know either.'

'Typical. Mustn't worry dear old Paddy.'

'It was really because of her husband's peace of mind.'

'I believe that . . . now. But Robbie was always different from me. I was much more experienced, even at nineteen. She didn't know a thing. An innocent. And Paddy was . . . Paddy. Even at twenty-four. On pleasure bent and damn the consequences. A womanizer, even at that age.'

The sad thing is, Nora thought, you can't accept that Robbie was the love of his life. 'Don't speak ill of the dead,' she said out loud with a smile but she had hurt Laure.

'I know, I know. But can you blame me for bearing a grudge? I was always second best.'

'But you loved him?'

'Who could resist Paddy? But, yes, I loved him. And I appreciate that Robbie was loyal to her husband and that he never knew Craig wasn't his. And Paddy could never understand why Robbie married someone else. And you took Robbie's place in his heart so there was no room for me.'

Nora looked at her mother's sad face. I could make it up to her, she thought, and said to cheer her up, 'I was intrigued by the site of Le Manoir. I learned from the library in Chartres it was destroyed during the War.'

'Yes, it was. Oh, we're a terrible lot, the Bouchiers! Shall we go up and see Daddy?'

Colonel Maguire was not in bed. He was sitting in a chair at the window in his dressing gown and slippers. He looked thinner, Nora thought, but he still had the fine skin and round rosy cheeks which his daughter used to have. His small bushy moustache followed the shape of his mouth giving him a constant doleful expression, sometimes pathetic, Nora remembered. He looked up shyly at her.

'Here's your granddaughter to see you, Daddy,' Laure said. 'Cheer you up.'

He didn't look cheered up. 'You shouldn't have brought her here when I'm not properly dressed . . . How are you, Nora?'

'Fine.' She went over to him and kissed his forehead. 'I'm glad you're feeling better. Mother and I have been having a long chat.'

He looked dryly at Laure. 'I can believe that.'

'She's forgiven me for dashing off, Daddy. And so have you, eh?' She plumped the cushion at the back of his head.

'Perhaps. Sit down, both of you.' He was still embarrassed. He'd been a devil for dressing up, Nora remembered, black tie always when he came to dinner. She supposed it was because of the Guards. 'There are plenty of chairs.'

'We'll sit on the window seat beside you and then you can hear us,' Laure said.

'Don't treat me like an old man. I'm not deaf.' He looked apologetically at Nora, and she smiled.

'I've been in France. At Le Manoir.' He gave her a brooding glance which she didn't understand. 'I had promised Paddy I'd go to Chantilly and see the Prix de Diane being run.'

His eyes brightened. 'The French Oaks! Something special about racing there. An aura. A *je ne sais quoi*.' He smiled and the moustache lifted up to show even white teeth, false.

Baby-face, Nora thought. I'll start visiting him regularly and get to know him really well, now that Paddy's gone.

'I stayed at Mother's house at Lapantelle. I mean, mine. She's given it to me.'

'Has she?' He looked enquiringly at Laure who nodded.

'Of course you know it's not the original place. Nothing

155

like it.' He had turned to Nora. 'It's a jerry building my wife, Blanche, had put up . . . before she died.' His face seemed to collapse.

'Don't distress yourself,' Laure said, bending forward and putting a hand on his arm. 'Actually it's quite a nice little house, ideal for a holiday home. Just to keep the site in the family.' She spoke placatingly.

'I don't want to see it.' He looked at Nora, dismissing the subject. 'And you've lost Paddy. Such a fine man in every way, and now both of us in the same boat. He couldn't have been that old.'

'Only fifty.' The moustache quivered and she said quickly, 'I've come to ask your advice, Grandfather. I'm selling Marchmount and there are two offers. I was telling Mother. . .' She stopped at the look of astonishment on his face.

'Selling Marchmount! In the name of God!' The same reaction as his daughter, only worse. Even his moustache seemed to straighten out, become more military. He straightened up, too. Colonel Maguire of the Royal Irish Guards.

'Well, you see, after Paddy . . . and I've decided to go to Trinity to study history.'

'Very commendable. Went there myself. Let women in now, do they? But what has that to do with selling Marchmount?'

'I'll buy a flat in Dublin.'

'Are you thinking of bearing children in a flat in Dublin!' He made it sound like a concentration camp. 'What happened to Liam?' Liam was a favourite of his. He'd had more patience with him than she'd had.

'He's a land surveyor now. He wants to go abroad.'

'But Marchmount would be there when he came home! Every young man wants to go abroad. I did, with my regiment. Korea, Suez, all over the place. World War

Two. Before that, mountaineering with Henri, Blanche's brother . . . that's how I met her. Nice apartment they had in Paris, the Bouchiers. . .' The moustache drooped. Laure's eyes told Nora to start talking.

'There's been no question of marriage, Grandfather. Our careers come first. I'll tell you about the offers I've had, then you can tell me—'

He held up his hand. 'Neither! Paddy would be dumb-founded! I'm not selling Lisborough. It's the family home just as Marchmount is. A home. Like an overcoat. I'd be bereft without it. It adds an extra dimension to life. I owe it to Lisborough not to throw it to the wolves. You should feel the same about your place. Of course, if you want to skedaddle off to Trinity and a miserable flat up a dark stairway with drunken oafs all around you when you have all this –' he waved at the view from the window – 'and the same goes for that Liam with his land surveying. Paddy thought the world of him even although he was the son of a jockey.' He moved his head impatiently on the cushion. 'He always said he had fine hands.'

'Yes, he has,' Nora said. She felt miserable. Maybe she had been headstrong, but that was Paddy's fault, but had she gone overboard, been autocratic?

'Houses like yours and mine . . .' – her grandfather wasn't finished – 'They're not merely houses, not merely homes, they are part of the country's economy. We help our country by running them, by keeping those miserable suburbs from overrunning everything in their way. And what places they are for children to be brought up in!' His moustache con-certina'd as he pursed his mouth. 'And it's not merely land in your case. There are the horses. Noble works of "Somebody up there –" ' he waved at the sky – 'Is there a finer sight than seeing them trotting out of the yard in single file on a crisp winter morning?' Nora looked at her mother, thinking at

157

least we both felt the same about the smells, but she was listening, it seemed, with approval. Perhaps you had to go away to come back, to appreciate what you had left.

'I had some great secret hiding places at Lisborough,' Laure said. 'The spinney and behind the horse boxes by the oak.'

'We have owls in the barn,' Nora said. 'Liam showed them to me one night. Scarey, but lovely. But you and I, Mother, we had no playmates. It was lonely not having any brothers or sisters.'

Her grandfather spoke, 'The Bouchiers don't like large families.' He looked peeved. 'I'm feeling tired, Laure. I think I'll get back into bed.' He looked sternly at Nora. 'It's your decision, of course. You own the place.' He, too, knew how to put the boot in.

She and her mother went downstairs together after the colonel had been tucked in. The audience was over. 'I've offended him,' Nora said.

'You could have asked his opinion first. He would have liked that. It's the way Paddy has brought you up. Yes, he would have liked to have a say.' She smiled. 'What he forgets is that if the Bouchiers don't have large families, they bring a lot of money to a marriage. Keeps Lisborough going.' Nora looked at her in surprise.

'But not Marchmount?'

'And Marchmount.' She nodded with a closed smile. 'Don't let it spoil your sleep. It never did Paddy's.'

Nora and her mother talked for a long time. They finished Cecilia's sandwiches and, since the coffee was cold, Laure opened a bottle of wine. There was a lot to explain and a lot to understand, phrases like, 'They're a terrible lot the Bouchiers,' and Grandfather's reluctance to talk about them, although he had said they had a nice apartment in Paris.

'Was it,' Nora asked, 'that he had met Grandmother's

brother, Henri, before the War at some mountain resort, say, Zermatt, which had resulted in an invitation to the Rue St-Honore apartment where he met Blanche, his future wife?'

Laure had agreed and said that since he was on active service she had remained in Paris with her parents.

Nora drove home eventually and carefully, since she was stuffed with Cecilia's sandwiches which had been washed down with a nice Sauvignon Blanc from the Lisborough cellar (courtesy of the Bouchier's no doubt).

She had a lot to ponder on. It would keep her busy for the rest of the afternoon.

Nineteen

June, 1940

The Bouchier family were having a confab in the large drawing room in their Rue St-Honore apartment. Blanche Bouchier, now Blanche Maguire, dark-haired, more confident than ever in her comparatively new status of married wife, was speaking, her eyes darting between her mother and father.

'I don't want to go to Cap D'Antibes, Papa, Maman! Buried down there when so much is going on. Poor Eddie! Henri is bound to be in the same fix too, hounded towards the Normandy coast. Goodness knows how they're faring! And you said, Maman, you were worried about Le Manoir as well with those wretched Tourniers deserting it. Let me go and see to it at least.'

Madame Bouchier was clearly influenced. 'There's something in what she says, Armand.' She appealed to Monsieur Bouchier who was fingering his spectacles with impatience while he listened. 'You know Henri, my dear. So fearless. At least Colonel Maguire (she still had difficulty with how to address her son-in-law) might be able to keep an eye on him. . .Oh, this dreadful war! Who would have thought . . .'

Monsieur Bouchier waved his spectacles in exasperation. 'Yes, yes, yes! But I've been sitting here listening to you women for ten minutes when I ought to be at l'Avenue de la

Bastille. Yesterday Monsieur Reynaud left for Tours and I should be at the office arranging for our evacuation, packing documents . . . Don't you realize it? Paris has been declared an open city!'

'He's right, Maman. The cafés are empty. So is the Ritz!'

Monsieur Bouchier threw up his hands. 'The Ritz, she says. If that were all!'

'So we don't matter, Armand?' Madame Bouchier put her handkerchief to her eyes.

'Of course you matter, *ma chère* Geneviève! If you didn't matter why else should I be sitting here when I ought to be seeing to the affairs of our poor beleaguered country? Can you understand what I'm saying! Everybody is fleeing. I've been ordered by the government to Tours but at the moment there isn't enough accommodation for families. We have a nice apartment at Cap D'Antibes looking on to that blue sea you love so much. And who knows, if the worst comes to the worst, the government will have to move further south as well. There is talk of Bordeaux. I can scarcely believe it has come to this.'

'How terrible!' Geneviève Bouchier's face was tragic. 'Beleagured is the only word. And you, my dear husband, responsible for so much.'

Monsieur Bouchier looked momentarily gratified.

'You go, Maman,' Blanche said. 'Papa worries about you. Take Alice with you and leave Cook to look after things here. She has a husband somewhere, hasn't she?' Blanche Maguire resembled her father, an official in the *Charge d'Affaires*, in her desire to get things settled. 'But there's Le Manoir. Our real home. You don't want that overrun because that miserable caretaker and his wife have scampered off to some relatives in the Auvergne, do you?'

Monsieur Bouchier sighed impatiently. 'At times I could wish we could scamper off to the Auvergne ourselves. The

Germans are soon going to engulf Chartres as well.' He looked at his watch. 'My dearest,' he appealed to his wife, 'get Alice to pack your bags and get off.'

'I'll drive you to the station then go on to Le Manoir and see to things there.' Blanche spoke with her father's authority.

'Do you think that will be safe? The roads will be packed with people fleeing south, your father has just told you, and the German army will be just behind, swallowing up everything in its path . . .'

'Just the time to go! I'll be out of harm's way at Lapantelle. The Panzers are never going to bother with a small place like Lapantelle. Besides, that's where Eddie will look for me. He'll know we've all cleared out of Paris.'

Monsieur Bouchier shook his head dolefully. 'Your poor husband may well be fighting at the Normandy coast for his life at this minute. Being harried into the sea. Not to mention our son!'

'I know, but Eddie said not to worry. He'd be all right. He's a colonel, remember. But if *you're* worried about me driving,' Blanche's tone was sweet, deferential, daughterly, 'what about Gérard Lezard? Couldn't you spare him to drive us? Maman and Alice to the station and then me to Lapantelle? He could take an official car, then your mind would be at rest. What do you say, Papa?' Her black eyes were limpid.

'Do you know Gérard?'

'Of course, we do, Papa. Don't we, Maman?'

He came to all our soirées, didn't he? Quite charming.' Even worried, Madame Bouchier was still capable of remembering charming young men. Now she drew herself up and raised her chin, the *grande dame*. 'Well, that's it settled. Women mustn't get in the way of affairs of state. I shall keep my worries about my dear son to myself and do as you say, Armand. And although I'd rather Blanche were with me, I'd be relieved if she found someone at Chartres to take care of Le Manoir. It was my parents' home. I'd hate to leave it unattended during these dreadful times.'

Blanche left her parents to make their goodbyes to each other. She went to her bedroom and began packing a bag for her stay at Le Manoir. In the kitchen she raided the larder, the frightened cook looking on, put pâté, bread, cheese, wine into a basket she found there.

'What a clever little schemer you are,' Gérard would say. It had been his distinctive profile, glanced at when he was escorting them to state functions, which had first attracted her; so daringly handsome, so aristocratic. That had only been the beginning of a teasing, light flirtation which was pleasant but unrewarding. His one goal in life was his career. Women were for mere philandering.

Because of her pique at Gérard, and encouraged by her parents, she had accepted Colonel Maguire's offer of marriage, an old friend of the family through his association with Henri in their student days. Eddie was just as aristocratic as Gérard, although without the same *élan*, but he represented security, and also in her parents' opinion had the steady temperament more suitable to their daughter's flightiness than someone like Gérard Lezard who had quite a reputation with women of a certain age as well as those of his own (if there was any possibility of them advancing his career).

'What a clever little schemer you are,' Gérard Lezard said as he drove away from the Gare de Lyon where they had seen off a tearful Madame Bouchier and her sour-faced maid, Alice. 'Look after Maman for me, Alice,' Blanche had said. For years she'd had the maid eating out of her hand with frequent bribes in the form of cast-off dresses, discarded jewellery and the like. Alice was a plain duck with a swan's aspirations. She thought Mademoiselle Blanche was the essence of *chic*.

'Look at that car,' Gerard said. 'Poor devils. They've pots and pans hanging on every door handle, and their mattress on the roof to protect them from bombs.'

'Poor souls.' The car was crowded, children mostly. 'But they say the Germans are quite polite if you speak to them.'

'It's easy for conquerors. I'll take that with a pinch of salt. But I shan't have time to stay, chérie. Needs must. I've got a hundred things to do. Tours won't be half bad, though. Quite a lively city.' He pointed with his chin. 'Versailles. That's seen plenty of conflict. Maybe the road won't be so busy now that's we're clear of the city. Look at that lot, trailing along on foot. And the pram. You can't see the child for all the stuff piled on top of it.'

'You'd think they could have planned it better, got a lift from someone. Still, that woman pushing the pram does look tired.' Good thing *she* hadn't become pregnant. Eddie had been careful.

'The road isn't as busy here, thank goodness,' Gérard said. 'Soon be Rambouillet, after that, Maintenon and then we're there. Good! I'll be back in Paris in a few hours.'

Blanche looked at his anxious face and thought, momentarily, what a selfish pig she was, manipulating this journey to Lapantelle simply to get him on her own. But it had been so dull in Paris, Eddie gone and possibly in danger, Maman worried stiff about Henri, as she was – he was a good sort, Henri – and Paris emptying. And now this road they were travelling on thick with traffic of all sorts, French and German. The Panzer troop carriers looked purposeful.

'There are a lot of German vehicles, Gérard? See this one. Packed with troops – how I hate that dull grey uniform! Don't tell me they're all making for Chartres next. That beautiful cathedral. I was confirmed there.'

'They'll stand and fight. They're too proud of their city. There's going to be a pitched battle and we're making straight for it. I heard some of the buildings have been razed to the ground already. *Le Boeuf* something or other.

'*Le Boeuf Coronné*. Bombed?'

'Destroyed by fire I should think. Same thing.'

Blanche made a decision. 'If that's the state of affairs I shan't have much chance of picking up caretakers for our house. Shall we turn back, Gérard? I'm sorry now I suggested it.'

His smile had no mirth in it. 'Impossible now. There's no way I could turn and go against all this. No, my dear Blanche, I'm afraid you're hoist by your own petard.' She caught his glance as he turned towards her, the smile . . . There was very little love in it. 'In for a penny, in for a pound. If I wait until it's late I should be able to get back to Paris under cover of the dark.'

'I'm sorry,' she said plaintively. 'I didn't realize. . .' Then tearfully she added, 'I'm very fond of Le Manoir. I have so many childhood memories, the surrounding countryside where we rode, Bois Richeaux, Maintenon, the chateau there, long summer days, parties, boating. Oh, I had some fine times. . .'

'I'll believe you.' She could hear the teasing in his voice. 'Well, let's hope it's still there.'

He was silent while he drove and Blanche took the opportunity to look again at his profile, that straight, well-defined nose, the fine mouth. And such lashes on a man. Such eyes for that matter, large, lustrous sometimes, mostly sharp, penetrating, intelligent eyes. He must have wanted to come. She tried to reassure herself. Otherwise he would have refused. But, then, Gerard wouldn't refuse Papa. He was too careful.

Why did I even start on this mad enterprise, she thought?

Boredom, shortage of male company? Lust? Eddie had introduced her to the joys of the connnubial bed, a sweet lover, too polite always, but sweet . . . Now, Gérard, he would be quite different, teasing, demanding, she closed her eyes on the remembered thrill. With Gerard it would be . . . exciting.

Maintenon, and the *carrefour*, but now there were even more troop carriers milling around. And our own troops. Plenty of black men. Ivory coast. Senegal. Supposing one of those officers barred their passage and asked them why they were travelling and where they were going? She was suddenly shaking. What a fool she'd been, a scheming fool! It *had* been bodies lying at the side of the road in that ditch. She had pretended not to notice. Gérard wouldn't miss them.

But hadn't they been told to flee Paris, and besides, Gérard represented the government – except that there was no government! That had transferred to Tours and Papa hadn't had much confidence in that move or that it would last for long . . .

And what about Eddie, fighting for his life on the Normandy shore? Perhaps even floating in the water riddled with bullets! Her eyes filled with tears at the thought. What would he think if he could see her now with a young man from Papa's department in the middle of what was going to be a pitched battle?

'There are the spires,' he said. 'So serene. It was worth coming for that.'

'Nothing else?'

'Who knows?' He negotiated the turning off for Lapantelle as if he had been coming here all his life. 'Let's hope we live to tell the tale.'

Twenty

The hall of Le Manoir was dark when they went in because all the doors opening off it were closed, but when Blanche switched on the light, nothing happened.

'I expect you'll find all your services are cut,' Gérard said. 'I'm not surprised.'

'There will be candles somewhere. Never mind. Come into the garden room.'

He followed her to the back of the house. In the room they entered, the large French windows showed the setting sun filtering through a small coppice at the end of an expanse of fields which seemed to run in a gentle slope towards the horizon. A soft pink light suffused the room, falling on mirrors which reflected it again on to pale sofas and chairs, a room for lounging in.

Blanche's spirits lifted. 'There's still enough light here to see. Oh, it's lovely to be back!' She unlocked the French windows and flung them open. 'There, isn't it beautiful?'

'Beautiful.' He came and stood beside her. 'Except for the noise. Don't you hear it?'

'Yes, I do.' Stupidly she had expected only the busy chatter of the evening birds, but instead there was a steady throbbing background of heavy traffic, of wheels turning endlessly on roads; quite unlike the usual peacefulness that lay on this part of the Beauce.

'Do you realize it?' Gérard turned to her. 'People fleeing,

the Germans advancing. I think we're in the middle of a war zone!'

'How awful!' But she was excited. 'That's why everything's cut off!'

'*Précisement!*' He spread his hands. 'Nevertheless, I'm terribly thirsty with all that dust driving. Could we have a drink, Blanche? Water would do.'

'I brought some wine and there's more in the cellar. We're not in danger, are we?'

'It seems far enough away meantime. Time for a drink, anyhow.'

'I can do better than that.' She smiled at him. 'A *bonne bouche* with your wine? I intended to give you a meal, but maybe the gas is off too. I'll see.'

She looked at herself in the hall mirror as she went past it towards the kitchen. Not bad. Her cheeks were flushed. She had always wanted to be pale and interesting, but never mind, and with the warmth in the car her hair was in damp ringlets on her brow. It was exciting, this element of danger.

Did Gérard find her attractive? Surely he must get a surfeit of the made-up ladies who came to the Embassy balls. Maman always said that since she had such a fresh complexion she shouldn't subdue it with powder, and certainly she had no need of rouge. Eddie liked her appearance. He was almost, well, worshipful at times, darling Eddie.

When she went into the garden room again, she found Gérard had stepped through the open windows and walked to the end of the garden. She could scarcely see him in the dark. He came towards her when she called to him. 'Your drink!'

'I'm sure I heard some guns firing,' he said. 'Cannons, maybe. And I saw lights.' He came into the room but stood at the open window. 'Do you hear it? A sharp kind of rattle. Which direction is that?'

'Maintenon.' That wasn't so far. 'Do you remember we came through the crossroads?'

'Listen!'

He was right. There was the distant heavy rumbling, an ominous sound, like thunder, but also the occasional sharper rattle. It wasn't ordinary traffic.

'Perhaps it will stop now that it's dark,' she said. 'Let's sit down and have that drink. I think we both need it.'

He was still looking towards the fields, his head tilted, listening, but he gave up and turning, shut the windows behind him. Once seated, with a plate of bread and duck pâté on his knee, a glass of wine at his elbow, he seemed relaxed.

'You're right,' he said. 'It will soon stop. Meantime,' he looked at her with a smile, 'this is very nice.'

'Thank you.' She dimpled. He was settling down now, and the noise was too far away to bother them. A glass of wine had been the answer.

'What are you going to do about your caretakers?' he asked. 'I doubt if you could venture to Chartres to make enquiries. Have you a car?'

'Yes. Papa always leaves a run-about in the garage. I can use that unless the Tourniers have taken it to make their get-away.'

'Shall we go and look?'

'Yes, perhaps we'd better.'

When they went outside there was the sudden frightening screech of several motor cyclists as they went roaring past the gates. She felt irritated rather than afraid at the peacefulness of the village being disturbed.

'Would you like me to close the gates?' Gérard asked.

'No, perhaps not. If you're going back soon . . .'

'I really must.'

The garage was empty.

'Can you believe it!' She was outraged. 'And Maman was

169

so good to them! They had all the produce of the garden while we were in the city and the use of the car, but she didn't expect they would steal it!' She remembered they had children. No, she mustn't think too badly of the Tourniers. These were exceptional times.

When they turned to go back they heard a far-away whistling, different from the general background noise. It seemed to ascend in an arc of sound, reach its maximum intensity and then descend in a dying fall.

'Chartres,' Blanche said.

'They're dropping bombs there. Run!' He took her hand and they made for the house. They were both panting when they collapsed on to one of the sofas in the garden room. It was quite dark now except for a glimmer of light from the large windows. The pinkness had gone.

'You're shaking!' He put an arm round her shoulders. 'I don't blame you. Let me fill up your glass.'

'Thank you, Gérard,' she said. 'Then I'll look for some candles.'

'I think we'll have to move to a different room. This one is too exposed with all that window space. But first a drink.'

'You won't be able to risk leaving in this,' she said, deliberately keeping the tremble in her voice. She ought to be more frightened, but there was still this strange excitement . . .

'It's imperative I get back, but you're right. We'll wait till it quietens down a bit.'

He gave her a glass of wine, and she drank it as if she had a thirst. A warm glow spread inside her. She drank again and held out her glass.

'A little more, please, Gérard. It's I who have a thirst now!' She laughed.

'What a girl! You'd better have some bread and pâté with it.' He filled the glass, set it on a side table with her plate beside it. On it was a half-eaten piece of bread, spread with pâté. She wasn't hungry.

'Strange, that bomb we heard,' Gérard said, sitting down beside her. 'You were right. It came from the direction of Chartres. Perhaps they're going to take it over, like Paris?'

'Not Chartres. There's the cathedral!'

'If it's in their way that won't matter. Your father will be wondering why I haven't come back by this time.'

'Oh, no! Papa would expect you to take care of me. Papa's like that. He wanted Maman and I to be looked after. He expected it of you.' A hint of her father's authority came through the words.

'So the evacuation of Paris doesn't matter in your eyes, not to mention the French government?'

'Women and children first!' The remark struck her as distinctly funny. She laughed and lifted her glass and drank from it. The pâté still didn't look appetising. She left it.

'I believe you're enjoying yourself.' He teased her.

'How could I? But we're safe here for the time being, so we might as well relax. Then when the noise stops you can get back to your beloved Paris.'

'I'm in a quandary.'

'In what way?'

'Well, if you can't see it, I shan't tell you.' He put his arm round her shoulders and kissed her cheek. 'Lovely Blanche,' he said. 'You're a temptress.'

'Do you think so?' There was the whistling sound again, muffled this time since they were at the back of the house, and this time she thought she heard voices. Things were being taken care of and Gérard's arm round her shoulders reassured her.

'People stirring in your village,' he said. 'Everything must be under control.'

He didn't sound worried and for some reason her thoughts

went to Eddie battling against the enemy. She felt a sudden deep, burning sense of shame.

'And don't worry about your mother and father,' he went on. 'He'll be in Tours by this time and she'll be whizzing along to Nice. They'll be unaware of what's going on here. In any case, they know you're in good hands.'

She knew he had turned towards her. 'Well, that's something,' she said, raising her face to his.

He bent down and kissed her.

'So lovely. If . . .' the rest of his words were drowned out by the roaring of a cannon followed by the whistling of bombs, sirens, voices again. He sprang up from the sofa.

'This room is dangerous! It's all windows! Come on, Blanche. You'll have to lead the way.'

'My room,' she said decisively. 'Follow me.' They were in the hall. She stopped, pointing. 'That's the drawing room. It will be just as bad. It's got to be my room. There's only one window. We'll see what's going on.'

He seemed doubtful, then: 'All right. Does it look out on to the gates?'

'Yes.'

'Lead the way.'

They ran upstairs and once when she stumbled, his hand was under her elbow. 'I should have brought the bottle,' she said, laughing.

'I think you've had enough.'

When they reached her room she plumped down on the bed. 'One way to get a man into my room,' she said, laughing. She imagined his eyebrows were raised at her, but it was too dark to see. He made straight for the window, but she couldn't hear any noise.

'Anything happening?' she asked. 'Or is the party over?'

'You're tipsy, you know.' He was still looking out of the window.

172

'Come beside me and have a rest.' He didn't reply, but she heard his footsteps and then he was lying beside her.

'Satisfied?' he said. 'What's this?' He had one of her furry animals in his hand.

'Can't see. It's probably Toby. My favourite.'

'Do you cuddle him at night?'

'For want of anything better,' she said. It's fear, she thought, making me behave like this. I've never been in the middle of an invisible war. There was still the background noise, the rumbling, staccato-interrupted noise of war.

She said, making an endeavour to sound practical, 'I'm worried about you, Gérard. How are you going to get back to Paris in the middle of all this? Listen! It's getting worse.'

The noise was continuous now, the firing of guns, men shouting, the occasional whistle of a bomb, but still seeming fairly far away.

'Well, we can't do anything about it, so we might as well enjoy it.' He was up on one elbow looking down at her. 'You really are beautiful. Why did you marry that foreigner when you could have had me?'

'Oh, oh!' She laughed. 'Why did you never ask me?' It was really quite delightful now, once you got used to the background noise. And the wine had loosened her tongue. She could say anything she liked. 'I've always admired you, you must have known, but you're so careful, Gérard! People say you're waiting for a rich widow with important connections who will further your career. Is it true?'

'Who, me?' He pretended astonishment, touching her nose and then her mouth with his forefinger. 'You were always surrounded by suitors and Henri told me I had to stay out of the way.'

'Henri! Why does he always interfere in my affairs? Typical brother!'

'I like you when your eyes flash,' he said.

173

He bent towards her, and at the same time there was a loud whistling noise then the dull thud of a bomb so near that her ears were filled with the reverberation, deafening her.

'My God!' He sprang up from the bed. 'That's in your garden! Or maybe an outhouse! What's on the other side from here?'

She was so terrified that it took her a second or two before she could get off the bed.

He repeated his question, shouting this time. 'What's on the other side of the house?'

'The other side?' She could hardly think. 'The drawing room, the study off it and then the garage!'

'It's the garage! I'm sure it's the garage!'

'Oh, Gérard,' she clung to him. 'What are we going to do? Are we trapped?'

'How do I know? I'll go downstairs immediately and find out. It could have been the . . .' He stopped. 'Do you smell burning?'

'I don't think so . . . Yes, I do.' It was in her nostrils, an acrid smell, making her cough. 'If it's the garage, there was nothing in it, Gérard. Remember we looked? When we went in . . .' She stopped, almost fainting at the thought.

'What is it?'

'We kept the oil tank for the central heating against its outside wall.' She was thinking clearly now. 'A large tank . . .'

They were both silent.

'We'll have to get downstairs right away,' he said quietly. 'Get out. Stand back. I'm going to open this door very very slowly in case . . .' He inched it open. She was beside him, looking . . .

The staircase was on fire, flames leaping so high that they could feel the heat on their faces.

'Get back!' When they were inside the room again he

174

closed the door, again very slowly, then leant against it. 'Must think what to do.'

'The window?' She spoke quietly.

'That's it. The window.' He went towards it, looked out and then turned to her. His face looked white in the darkness.

'What is it?' Her feet seemed stuck to the floor.

'The whole house is in flames. I can see them leaping at the side. It'll take no time to spread. This is our only means of escape.'

'It's too high to jump.'

'One storey. Let me think. Could we make a rope with the bedclothes?'

It struck her as comical, but she knew that if she laughed it would turn to weeping. 'Perhaps. It's been done.' There must have been laughter in her voice because he shouted at her.

'Stop that! God, what a fool I was to agree to this at all! I'm as bad as you are . . .'

'Listen!' She held up her hand silencing him. There was the loud sound of sirens and then men's voices, very near.

'You look out,' he said, surprising her.

Blanche went to the window and tried to wrench it open. In the darkness she could see a group of men in the front garden with lights. She heard a man's voice, shouting. '*Il y a quelque un?*'

'Gérard!' Her voice was suddenly like her father's. 'Open this window for me! It's stuck.' He didn't reply, and when she called, 'Gérard!' again, he came forward reluctantly, and grasping the handles at the foot heaved it open. She leant out and called, '*C'est moi! Madame Maguire!*'

'*Qui?*' A man's rough voice shouted.

She realized he wouldn't recognise the name. '*Mademoiselle Bouchier!*'

'*Ah, oui! Bien!* We have a ladder. You and the other person

175

must come down it immediately! Le Manoir is blazing at the garage side. It will spread quickly to you!'

She saw the ladder, held by someone. The man who had been speaking came up a few steps and held out his hand.

'*N'avez pas peur!* You first!' She turned to Gérard who was standing out of sight.

'What a relief! I'll go first and then you . . .'

He waved his arm dismissively. 'You go on. I'll get downstairs myself.'

'But it's blazing?' She was dumbfounded.

'Isn't there another staircase?'

'*Mademoiselle Bouchier! Dépêchez-vous!*' She heard the man's voice.

'Oh God!' she said. And turning quickly, 'Yes, there's another one. At the back of the house. The servants. But you might not reach it. The landing will be blazing.'

'I'll manage. On you go! *Vite! Vite!*'

She watched him open the door, slowly, and disappear, seeming to be drawn . . .

She collapsed into the arms of two soldiers when she reached the ground. 'There was another person, wasn't there?' one of them asked.

She couldn't speak for sobbing. She heard one man say to the other. 'Hysterical. I could have sworn I saw another person . . .'

Twenty-One

1989

Nora had previously intended to go to Dublin to see about her history course, but she had put it off until the afternoon because her mother had said she would like to come to Marchmount in the morning.

'I've got to get it over with,' she'd said, 'but I don't mind telling you I'm dreading seeing the old place. So full of memories.'

Promptly at ten she arrived on an old hack from her father's stable. 'It's the only one left,' she said, dismounting. 'Daddy's given up riding.'

'Maybe that's wise.' She saw her mother looked tired, her eyes dark-ringed in her sallow face. 'Come in and see the old place,' she said, smiling. 'I really shouldn't be saying that to you. It's yours as much as mine.' They went up the steps together.

Laure stood in the hall looking around. 'Just as I remembered it. Do you still keep great fires here? Paddy liked it lit every morning and kept going into the evening.'

Yes, Nora thought, yes . . .

'Not in summer, and I've no help. Mhairi's looking after an old uncle, and I was in France, but, yes, if I'm here I will indeed. It needs a fire.'

Her mind went back to the evenings when she and Paddy

had sat together here, but the thought didn't disturb her now.

'Will you come into the kitchen while I make some coffee for us?' And then, laughing she added, 'I feel strange, Mother, inviting you like a guest, you know. As if I had displaced you.'

'I displaced myself. It's I who should feel sorry. I've broken the back of it now, I hope. Come on, then, let's go into the kitchen.' She linked her arm through Nora's and she felt a sense of comfort and rightness. This is how it should be, she thought. Maybe if this Mr Dexter died she'll come back to Lisborough and we'll be really good friends.

'Ah, yes,' her mother said when Nora was busy at the stove. She looked around. 'Ah, yes. Well, I'll say Mhairi kept it nice. Are you a tidy girl?'

'Tidy enough. But I don't like housework much. Mhairi was far too competent for me to be needed. But Paddy liked me at the dinner table when he had guests. Well, here we are.' She brought the coffee pot over to the table and reached up to the shelves above for the cups and saucers.

'She's been careful with the china. Not a smasher. These are the same. Gold-rimmed white for the kitchen. I remember them.'

'Yes, she was competent in many fields.' Make what you like of that, Mother. 'Would you like some biscuits?'

'No, I never eat them. I have to watch my figure. You seem to do that.'

'Oh, yes. I'm like the jockeys around here. Eat sparingly. Keep the weight down. That was always Paddy's teaching, although he liked a nice table for the guests. Good food and wine.'

'The things of the flesh. Ah, that's nice coffee. Strong. How I like it.'

'I'm glad.' Nora lifted her own cup. 'But I still feel as if you were a sister, or a friend who's turned up after a long time, not a mother.'

'Maybe that's a better arrangement. God, how I feel Paddy around this house! I wouldn't be surprised if he came walking in, although maybe he wouldn't have come into the kitchen.'

'Maybe not, but he was always down at the yard in the morning. How's Grandfather feeling today?' she asked. Always Paddy.

'Pretty good. He's like most men. Likes a bit of pampering. Have you still got the orangery?'

'Oh, yes. Aidan's pretty good at keeping it nice with the plants he's cosseted. Paddy and I didn't sit in it a lot.'

'He did when we had guests. Shall we join the ladies? kind of thing. He liked to bring the men there with their brandy and cigars. What a stickler for tradition he was! Hidebound. He could behave as he liked, but women had to be conventional. Did you know that?'

'Only recently. Since I met Robbie Clancy. But he could charm the birds off the trees, you must admit.' Her voice broke. 'I loved him. I know he loved me.'

'He deserved your love. I had to earn it. Oh, for God's sake, don't let's get sentimental.' She laughed. 'I was like one of his flighty horses, wayward. But then he didn't love me.'

'I don't know about that. All I know was that he took your place and I was happy with him.' Nora felt that was harsh, but it was said.

Her mother shrugged in acceptance. 'Ah, well, it's past now, and he's gone.' Her smile was feeble. 'Daddy was really pleased to see you. Men of all ages like pretty girls. He says I've to ask you for lunch. He's coming downstairs today.'

'Liam's coming in the evening, but yes, thank you, I'd like to. I'm driving to Dublin in the afternoon, I think, to fix up about some classes.'

'I can't believe in this, somehow. Do you really mean to become a student, at your age?'

'What would you rather I'd be doing?'

'Getting married, I suppose. All the Bouchiers married young.' Her chin tilted.

'That's not the whole object of my existence.'

'This Liam. He was only a lad when I left, following his father all over the yard. A grand jockey. Thrown and killed, wasn't he? Is Liam small like him?'

'No, tall and handsome, too handsome, but his chin saves him. Determined. The girls were always buzzing round him but he was aloof. And his eyes. He listens with them. Sometimes I feel I know him too well to be, you know, romantic.'

'If you went to bed with him you'd soon feel romantic if he's all that handsome. Have you?'

'That's my business.' Nora laughed. 'I couldn't have said that to you if you'd been here all the time, but—'

'I've to earn my place? Ah, well, I'm not back yet. There's Norman, and he's taught me what real love is. But when he goes, I'll come back to Lisborough to look after your grandfather. My heart's still in Ireland.'

'Not France?'

'Half and half. My mother didn't live to be old. I'll probably be the same.'

Nora looked at the strained, sallow face and the rush of love was there again, but how could she spring at her and throw her arms round her neck? It would take time. Her head was lowered, she was toying with her spoon.

'Mother,' she said gently, 'it must be distressing for you here, at first. If you've finished your coffee let's have a walk around.'

She looked up gratefully. 'I'm being stupid. This place is too much for me. Too much of Paddy.' She got to her feet. '*Alors, je suis prête.* Do you keep up your French?'

'*Bien sûr.*' Nora got up too, thinking, It's the same as on one of Starlight's flighty days when your hands were what mattered: gentle, coaxing, loving, decisive. 'I'm not surprised it's a bit much for you. You've had a long trip here, and then Grandfather, and your husband being ill – a lot on your mind. Let's go to the yard for some fresh air.'

'And some horsey smells?' She laughed, seemingly more at ease. 'Ah, but you've got the right way with you, I'm thinking.'

And when they were in the fifty-yard square at the back of the house, she stood, looking around, her eyes on the weathered brick, the ivy-covered clock tower, all in good repair. 'Paddy's strictures haven't been forgotten. Spick and span.'

They chatted to the stable lads who were grooming the two thoroughbreds still in the loose boxes.

'Nice to see you back, Mrs Malone.' Sammy's monkey face was stretched in a grin. 'My, Paddy is missed around here!'

'Falling to pieces, is it?' Laure smiled.

'Liam was the boy for managing things, but he had other ideas. Well, I don't blame him.' And to Nora he said, 'A fine seat your mother had, Miss Nora, by God she had.'

'There are only two horses here?' Laure asked when they walked on.

'The owners have no fixtures for them. We're stabling them for the time being.'

'And you've no trainer?'

'No. Since Paddy died we've had several men but they haven't been much good. I told you about the two Liam's found for me, but –' she shook her head – 'no, if he'd been staying on, but he's not interested. He's going abroad.'

'Pity. Sammy's no good?'

Nora shook her head again. 'Sammy's our standby. He

181

just doesn't have it up here –', she touched her head – 'but he'd be miserable if he weren't living with horses.'

'It won't do,' Laure said.

'What do you mean?'

'Marchmount was known as a place of quality. You should be at your busiest, just now. Races every week. Here and in England and France. You should have persuaded Liam to stay.'

They were leaning on the white-painted fence looking away across the fields to the spinney. It was a grey morning, soft, like a veil. Something gleamed on the road at the side of the fields, a car mirror, a flash in the greyness. But the birds were noisily busy in the tall sycamores and the pigeons were fluttering over the yard, picking the seeds from the horses' droppings. The owls would be hiding in some dark place in the barn.

'His heart isn't in it, Mother. He loves horses, he's good with them and he's the type of person that anything he takes on he does well. Everybody likes him. You heard Sammy. But the racing world doesn't appeal to him. He's not built for the racing chat, the eternal talk of horses, studs, form, bets, the skulduggery that he's seen going on. His mind's set on exploring the world, how it's made up, how it works, its essence . . . Oh, I can't explain, but I know how he feels. It can be a very comfortable prison, this, but it's a prison. There is only one topic of conversation and that is horses. They're beguiling, of course, beautiful animals, but sometimes mean and nasty and difficult to deal with. He doesn't want it.'

'Well, you seem to know what he wants. And it isn't you?'

Nora shrugged. There would be no more confidences for the time being.

Again, when they went through the gate in the yard and on to the path leading to the spinney, her mother linked arms with her. The feeling of love was there strongly, a newly-born love for a newly-born mother, or at least a new experience for her to have one. I managed, she thought, but being brought up by Paddy left a lot out. The feminine touch.

'When I go back,' Laure said, 'you should try and have some chats with your grandfather. He'd be flattered.'

Again Nora felt a pang of regret. How self-centred she had been all those years. Only Paddy.

'He's never mentioned your mother.'

'Blanche? No, well, you can understand that. He would have been so proud of his lovely young bride, daughter of a rich French family with a pied-à-terre in Paris and the same on the Côte d'Azur. Le Manoir was the family home.'

'And then her early death. What was the cause?'

'Some chest complaint, I think. Pneumonia. Mostly guilt. It eats into the soul.'

They were both silent as they came out of the spinney and got on to the road.

'A tragedy,' Nora said at last. 'You had a much worse upbringing than me. At least I knew you were alive.'

'There was that. No wonder I went off the rails after I married Paddy. Yes, I was lonely as a child, only Cecilia to talk to. Daddy was a remote figure then, always immersed in army business which took him away from home, and then, like you, I was at school in Paris. With Robbie. And it was I who introduced her to Paddy at Chantilly – we'd been neighbours back home – and well, you know the rest. It wasn't surprising I hopped off with that clod, Kevin, and left you and Paddy. He was never faithful to me. Did you know that?'

'I know now.' And then. 'I'm still thinking about what you told me yesterday, and the behaviour of that Gérard.'

'Yes. And he met his death, poor soul.'

'He couldn't face being found in your mother's bedroom so he flung himself into the flames rather than escape by the window?'

'I don't think that's the whole way of it. When he learned from my mother that there was another staircase he saw *that* as a means of escape. He'd jump into his car, drive to Paris, and no one would know he'd been there.'

'But he would have been stopped! There would have been soldiers at the front of the house where his car was. He would have been seen . . .'

'He took that risk. Being a diplomat, he would think he could talk his way out of it. On Embassy business. His charred body was found on the upstairs landing.'

Nora bit her lip. 'Dreadful.' She was silent as they walked. 'Who told Grandfather?'

'She did. Blanche.'

'When she went back to Ireland?'

'Yes. He got injured getting out of Dunkirk – a cracked pelvis – he was invalided for a time, then given the job of training his regiment for their eventual assault on the beaches, but he never saw active service again. He went back to Lisborough and she was waiting for him there. I was born in 1943 – the living proof of the reconciliation.' She smiled.

'And then she died not so long after?'

'I was about five. I think she never got over that experience at Le Manoir and *le scandale*. She felt it killed her parents, but perhaps that wasn't strictly true. Henri was killed at Dunkirk.' They walked on without speaking for a time.

'Now I can understand the large gates at Le Manoir,' Nora said.

'Yes. Blanche had the smaller house built after the war, just to preserve the site.'

Nora put an arm round her mother's shoulders. 'If I were you, I'd get back to your husband right away. Grandfather will be all right. I'll keep an eye on him. I've been selfish there.'

'Don't *you* start apologizing!' They both laughed.

184

Laure looked better when they were back at the yard and Nora was helping her to mount.

'I feel much lighter after getting rid of all that,' she said, smiling down at Nora.

She looked great on a horse. Aristocratic was the word. Miss Autocrat, Paddy had called *her*, she remembered. Had he been thinking of the Bouchiers?

Twenty-Two

Liam arrived at the house about nine o'clock that evening. 'Sorry I'm late,' he said. 'Trouble at the yard. Joe reported one of the thoroughbreds was lame and I had to wait until the vet came. It was nothing serious, but –' he looked at her – 'the responsibility is on you.'

'I know that, Liam.' They were eating in the kitchen, food that Nora had taken out of the freezer which his mother had kept stocked.

'We'll talk about it later, but' – she had to tell him – 'guess what, my mother has been here today!'

'Your mother? Mrs Malone?'

'Yes. *Quel surprise*, as the French say.'

'Do they? That was great for you. What brought her back? A guilty conscience?'

'Don't be hard on her. My grandfather has been ill and her husband told her she must fly over and see him. He's very ill himself. It was decent of him.'

'Very decent.' He smiled at her. 'How did it feel seeing her after so long?'

'Peculiar, and yet normal. Blood is thicker than water. One minute I was thinking, who is this stranger, and the next was saying to myself, but this is my mother! Most of the time I thought of her as a sister. I suppose that may be the state most girls of my age reach.'

186

'Possibly. She was French, wasn't she? What was their family name?'

'Bouchier.'

'I remember Paddy telling me once that he liked being connected to a French family. And I remember her. She was dark, and . . . different, beautiful – not bad for a ten-year-old! She made other women seem ordinary; even my mother.'

'She's lost a lot of that. She's had to nurse her husband whom she seems to be very fond of, and in some ways she's an unhappy woman. Regrets, I suppose. All her energy seems to have been thrown into devoting herself to him, almost as a penance. She says she'll come back to Lisborough when he's dead.'

'Does she? Well, that would be good for you. Nice to feel you're no longer an orphan. I thought you might when Paddy died, but now that's she's back in the picture I'm glad for you, really glad.' He leant back in his chair. 'The inner man is replete. That was one of my mother's offerings, wasn't it? I know them all.'

'Yes, I took it out of the freezer.' She reflected that he never showed much enthusiasm when his mother was mentioned. Had he suspected that she and Paddy had been sleeping together? Except for his physique, he didn't resemble her. He had his father's colouring and looks, but his mother's height.

'We'll go and sit in the hall,' she said. 'Mother was reminding me how much Paddy liked being there, especially in the evenings . . .' She looked away, biting her lip.

'You still miss him,' he said, rising and standing behind her, his hands on her shoulders.

'Yes, at certain times. Evenings, at the hall fire, cosy . . .'

'Paddy was a character.' The pressure of his hands was comforting. 'He's left an impression on everyone, an imprint. Maybe that's immortality.'

187

'It could be. When I was in Chartres and in the cathedral, I lit a candle for him. He could have been standing beside me, I felt him so close.' She sighed and got up. 'I'll make the coffee. Will you take a bottle of whisky from the drinks cupboard? That was what he liked. It should have been brandy, I suppose.'

'He was a real Irishman. Would it be brandy in France?'

'Cognac. Just as good in France. To each his own. Lead on Macduff. Take glasses. I've got the coffee.'

They settled themselves comfortably in the sofa in front of the hall fire. The dogs followed them, chose their places on the hearthrug and stretched out. Liam had thrown on a few more logs and they were crackling and spitting as they flamed. Costain, the older dog, looked up irritably and shifted his position.

Costain was Paddy's dog and he had seemed to grow old and grumpy when Paddy died. Always Paddy, her mother had said when she was here this morning. Nora sipped her coffee looking into the heart of the fire, once again imagining his eyes that evening when they had grown hot and he had kissed her mouth . . . Of course he was a charmer, anyone in a skirt.

How was it with Liam? she wondered, watching him as he poured whisky into the glasses in front of them, long-limbed, and his satisfying set of the fair head on his shoulders. He had a presence too.

His grey eyes turned on her as if he knew she was watching him. 'You're sad tonight. Take a good sip of that whisky. It'll do you good.'

'Thanks. My mother felt Paddy here.'

'He's built into the house. When you sell it, you sell him too.'

'Oh, Liam, you prophet of doom!' She laughed. 'I was invited to Lisborough for lunch today.'

'What did they have to say about selling Marchmount?'

'Grandfather was dead against it. Tradition, all that kind of thing. Well, you would expect that from him; army men are the most traditional of people. Dyed in the wool.'

'That's him dismissed. And Mrs Malone?'

'Ambivalent, I think. She's French, remember, and her allegiance must be divided, except that her first concern is to look after her husband and then Grandfather until he pops off.'

'It doesn't sound like the Mrs Malone I remember. Can leopards change their spots?'

'We'll see.' She sipped her whisky and the firelight danced and she thought, Is there anything nicer in the world than sitting in this shabby old hall? And that's tradition.

'She has a family home too. I wonder if it was like this – traditional? But aren't all family homes the same; full of trophies of the past which no one has the courage to get rid of?'

'Is that a rhetorical question, Miss Malone?'

She gave him a punch on the shoulder.

'Hey, watch it!' He put down his glass.

'She told me an amazing story about her mother, Blanche Bouchier.'

'Hadn't you heard it before?'

'Not from Paddy, and don't forget she skedaddled when I was ten. Had I been closer to Grandfather he might have told me, but somehow he always seemed to be Paddy's pal . . . I'll visit him oftener now.'

'He's a decent old codger behind that furry moustache. Like a terrier. Snap, snap! Go on. What was the story?' He settled back again.

'Well, my grandfather was with his regiment during the War, the Irish Guards, and Blanche, his wife, was living in her parents' apartment in Paris while he was away. Actually, it was the worst time, the Allied Army retreating, the Germans advancing. They occupied Paris then.'

'1940'

'Right. Blanche's father, Armand, got alarmed, and wanted his wife to go with Blanche to their apartment in Cap D'Antibes. He was on the staff of the Embassy and they had been directed to proceed to Tours.'

'So?'

'Blanche dug her heels in and said she'd rather go to the family home at Lapantelle, a village near Chartres. Her excuse was that her husband, Grandfather, would be more likely to look for her there than in Cap D'Antibes.'

'Quite sensible.'

'Grandfather's name is Eddie, by the way. What he didn't know, was that Blanche engineered that she would be driven to Le Manoir, by an aide of her father's whom she fancied.'

'True to type.'

'Well . . . anyhow, something terrible happened. When Blanche and this Gérard Lezard were in her bedroom, a stray bomb fell on the house and set it on fire. She escaped but he was burned to death.'

Liam sat up to look at her. 'God! Burned to death! What a shock for the colonel!'

'You can say that again, especially as he was fighting for his life at Dunkirk. Fortunately, although he had a cracked pelvis, he recovered but never saw active service again. He and Blanche were reunited at Lisborough and my mother was born there, in 1943.'

Liam refilled their glasses and lay back again. 'We don't know we're alive. It explains in a way why your mother went off with Kevin. It was in the blood.'

'I don't think that was the reason.' She lifted her chin. She wasn't going to mention Paddy's unfaithfulness. Yet.

Liam turned his glass in his hand. 'I should think if you were going to follow in the Bouchier tradition you would have done it by this time.'

'How do you know I haven't?'

He looked taken aback. 'You're not the type.'

'So you think.' She let one side of her mouth go up. As you know, I was staying at Le Manoir when I was in France. I had an . . . interesting time. It's no longer a manor, just a holiday cottage. I believe Blanche had it built to preserve the site.' She let her mouth lift again, suitably inscrutable. 'I'll tell you what happened there sometime.' She never would in a hundred years. Richard Trant was buried along with Le Manoir.

He took hold of her shoulders and she saw anger in his eyes. 'Don't be a bloody tease. I don't know you like that.'

The anger was so intense that she turned away.

'Don't get so heated up.' Her head swam. She put down her glass.

'Sorry.' He breathed deeply. 'All the same, I think both Paddy and the colonel were quite pleased with their French connection.'

'So they should have been. The Bouchiers were very rich.' She thought of her mother, remembered the strained face, the sallow skin, no effervescence. Even the hair had undergone a metamorphosis which didn't suit her. 'You wouldn't recognize my mother now. All the fire's gone.'

'That's a shame. More whisky?'

'No, thanks. My head is swimming a little. It's dangerous. I've a lot of decisions to make about Marchmount.'

'I see that. So many considerations. For instance, if the owner of Constancy, that's the thoroughbred that's gone lame, gets wind of it he won't be well pleased. Marchmount has a name for quality.'

'My mother said that.'

'It might be better to close the stables than risk ruining its reputation.'

Nora sighed. 'I didn't like those prospective buyers who came. It would depend on the young man getting a good trainer, and you know the trouble we had, and the brothers were too grasping, the wrong type.'

'I've another suggestion. I meant to tell you this right away.'

'Someone else?'

'Yes. This man wrote to me.' He felt in his pocket. 'I have the letter in the car. I'll go and get it.'

'No, don't go. Just tell me.'

'His owner is giving up. He had quite a big stud near Newmarket, but no family to carry it on. The man who wrote – he had phoned when you were away and Sammy had given him my address – is in Dublin on holiday and making a few enquiries seemingly. He'd heard the rumour about March-mount. He says he believes in quality, that he just wouldn't go anywhere, but Paddy had a good reputation.'

'That sounds promising.'

'We met for a drink. He seems the right type: fiftyish, quite debonair, divorced. Very knowledgeable. He had good recommendations from his former employer. He has a fancy for living in Ireland, says something in the water bred the best horses.'

'He's thinking of Irish whisky.'

'Maybe he meant the grass.' He laughed. 'You'd like him. I should have told you right away but the news about your mother and her mother scuppered me. He said he could build up Marchmount again; that he thought it was right for him.'

'He sounds right for us. Except he doesn't want to buy?'

'He said not, but I'm not so sure. He's cautious. I thought you could offer him a three months' trial on either side. That would give you time to sort out your own affairs.'

'I enrolled today at Trinity. I start in September.'

'Well, it's all tied up. And my time's up too. I go off tomorrow.'

'Tomorrow!' She was speechless. 'Why didn't you tell me?'

'I did. It's on your desk. I go to a conference in Montana with another bloke, and we work afterwards for a large company there. I'll be away three months.'

'Oh, Liam!' She was devastated. 'Yes, I knew about the conference, but I thought you came home and then went away again, afterwards . . .'

He shook his head. 'No. It's a *fait accompli* as they say in France.'

'Cut that out!' She was suddenly furious. She met his eyes and they seemed to have gone darker. There was no hint of a smile in them. His announcement had been deliberately low-key, she recognized that. It was the way he would always handle things.

They were both silent. She stared into the fire, watching the glowing embers, seeing in the bed of ash the large tract of land which was Montana, on the other side of the world.

'I have never been to Montana,' she said. 'Of course, there's my half-brother in Boston . . .' She felt him tense. 'I meant to tell you more about him, but there's been so much to talk about. And then my mother's home is in Arizona. Is that near Montana?'

'Much further south . . . Did you say . . . your half-brother?'

'Later.' She waved the question away. 'It's exciting for you, going to Montana.'

'Yes, exciting.' He was uneasy. 'I'm Irish enough to want to see what took so many Irishmen to the US of A, leaving the ould country for the new . . .'

She was sitting straight, steeped in misery, too much even to tease any more. He didn't speak. He wasn't going to ask again about Craig. He knew her through and through; he knew that she would only tell him when it suited her. And why should she be steeped in misery? she asked herself. Hadn't she enrolled at Trinity? Wasn't she a steady girl? Everyone thought so. She had to go about her life in an independent way, not give in to this deep, miserable misery that lay like an undigested meal in the pit of her stomach. Bejasus, she thought, I'm in love with this man. I don't just love him, as I always thought, I want him, to hold him close, to prevent him going anywhere away from me, Montana or anywhere else.

'I know what I'll do,' she said. 'What's this man's name you met?'

'Gerald Prosser. Called Gerry. I said you would ring him if you were interested.'

'I am.' It was easy once you became decisive. It was the hanging about, the indecision that wore you out. She'd concentrate on this for the time being. Marchmount was a wonderful property and Gerry Prosser would take it in hand. 'That's it,' she said. 'I've said to my mother I'll keep an eye on Grandfather. He's nearly eighty now, and frail. I'll go to my classes every day then look in on him every afternoon, give that Cecilia what-for if she isn't taking care of him properly. I'll give this Gerry three months to prove himself, and then if that's going well and my studying . . .'

'You're ready to clear out?'

'That's it. I feel better about things now, Liam.' How beautiful he was. She stopped talking because his eyes were on her, holding her, pinning her down. She tried to look like herself.

'Why are you looking at me like that?' she demanded.

'I wondered if there was any space for me in there with all that planning?'

'Don't forget' – she was haughty – 'you did all yours

without consulting me. There was no room in there for me.'

'I told you I was going. You don't even read what I put in front of you. I've told you often that you were the only girl for me.'

'Plenty of men have said that!' She didn't know what she was doing or saying. As if all those callow youths at county balls, who said when dancing, 'Where have you been all my life?', meant anything at all. Liam was silent.

She stared into the fire and slowly remembrance of that evening came back to her when Paddy had kissed her mouth while his eyes held her . . . and it didn't mean a thing. He was a womanizer, that was the nub of it. He would never in a thousand years have . . . She turned and looked at Liam. He was looking at her. His eyes were like Paddy's had been, hot, moist, as if they had absorbed the heat of the fire.

'What are you staring at?' she said.

'You. You're autocratic.' His voice was bitter: 'No wonder Paddy called you that. Now I know you've inherited it from the Bouchiers; the belief that the world spun round you not you round the world, that you were the one! Has it ever occurred to you to question my reluctance?'

'No, not particularly.' She raised her chin. 'You were always single-minded, a do-er, wrapped in your own wonderful career, far from horses.'

'I was the son of a jockey, my mother worked for you, I have had snide remarks made before now about you and knowing which side my bread was buttered on. "You're all right, Jack" kind of stable talk. It's not the horses I objected to!'

'Do you worry about that sort of thing?' She was genuinely interested.

'What do you think? I wanted to get away from it, to make my own career, be somebody on my own, not a yard lad.'

She saw it. Of course, she knew the rough talk that went

on, but that was just his bad luck. They were all living in a natural environment where they tended animals and sometimes behaved like them. Paddy had been a gentleman, but when she had left the dinner table to him and his friends, she had often heard the raucous laughter and knew that the conversation was not much above animal level. She wouldn't have been shocked, but they would have expected her to be. She suddenly remembered Richard Trant and thought, Another animal . . .

She turned to Liam and said, 'Why don't you kiss me goodbye, then?'

He smiled at her slowly, his eyebrows raised. 'Why don't I? Wasting all this time.'

It began as a friendly kiss, and then it was the kiss of a healthy male: rough, demanding. Just when it might have reminded her of Richard Trant he apologized and became tender and loving and spoke for a long time about his ambitions and his dreams.

'Only you,' he said. 'It's always been only you.'

He was right, of course. It had always been there in the background, sometimes pushed aside, sometimes dismissed, but always in the wings. Nearly all her life there had been Liam, helping her, supporting her, working for her, but also for himself, for his future life, his own work, for some expression of his own character. For his self-respect.

She sighed deeply. 'I'm going up to bed,' she said. 'Why don't you come too?' Miss Autocrat, she thought. Well, that was her temperament, he could like it or lump it.

But when he was lying beside her it was she who became the suppliant. She was deeply moved, deeply surprised. I haven't lived until this, she thought, and then, But I have, only now my life has meaning. He kissed her as if she were the yard well and he was drinking from it.

'We've wasted a hell of a lot of time,' he said.

When they were having a cup of tea before he left, she felt tired but not sad that it was goodbye for three months. She had to get used to so much happiness.

'I'm glad I invited you,' she said.

'I'm glad I accepted the invitation. Will you pine for me?'

'I think I will.' Shyness was foreign to her. 'You've always been there but now it's different. I thought I was having an exciting time in France, but it's nothing compared with this. Almost too much.'

'There's an inexhaustible supply. I reckon it'll last us all our lives.'

'That's good to know.' She tapped his nose. 'Seducer!'

'What a nerve!' He grinned at her. 'And then there's this Gerry Prosser. He's staying at the Shelbourne. Don't get carried away by him.'

'That can only happen once to me. It's happened.'

'Maybe there's a right time. Maybe we were too immature.'

'Were you really waiting till I asked you?'

'Something like that.' His grin was beguiling and it was difficult to let him go.

But she was an independent woman, she told herself. Her affairs were going to be in apple-pie order from now on with the help of Gerry Prosser, and she had found out what was missing in her life, like lifting a veil.

She smiled beatifically on her lover, Liam. 'Oh,' she said, full of happiness.

'Should I have told you how beautiful you are and how I love your red hair?' Craig added.

'Copper.'

'Copper-red, and that quirky smile of yours . . .'

'Leprechaun, it's called. There's no point in praising me when you know you're far more beautiful than I am.'

'So, tell me all about Craig, then,' he said, not denying it.

She started to tell him, but he had what she thought of as a transcendent look as if he wasn't quite taking it in.

She wept when he left. It was hard luck to have known such joy and have to wait three months to have it repeated.

Twenty-Three

She hardly recognized this new tremulous Nora who couldn't concentrate without thinking of Liam, who found herself smiling for no reason, who started to perform some mundane task and stopped in the middle of it to appreciate the slow thrills running through her when she thought of him, of his hands on her. What a lot of time we've wasted, she thought. He had said that too.

He telephoned her from the airport and she felt girlish and shy and stupid, then laughed at herself and apologized. 'I don't know what I'm saying this morning. You've upset the apple cart all right. I'll have to take myself in hand.'

'I'd like to see you like that.'

'Oh, I'll be back to normal by the time you get back.'

'And then I'll upset the apple cart again. Now you know how I've felt for years.' Silly lovers' talk.

She took herself in hand and telephoned the number he had given her for Gerry Prosser. She liked the sound of his voice and invited him to come and see her that afternoon. He didn't hesitate in accepting, which pleased her.

'Three o'clock?'

'Three o'clock. I'll look forward to that.'

She telephoned her mother afterwards and asked how her grandfather was. She was getting more used to having them both in her life.

'Yesterday was a bit too much for him. He's staying in his

199

room today. I'll sit with him some of the time, but how about you coming for dinner? The new maid here, Maureen, is proving herself to be quite a good cook.'

'Is she? Liam's gone away now.' She had to bring him into the conversation.

'Yes, you told me he was going. How long for?'

'Three months. And he's given me the address of a man who's interested in working at Marchmount. Liam thinks he might buy, but I thought if I gave him a trial for that time, we'd see how he turned out.'

'Would that matter if he didn't intend to buy?'

'I'll see what he says. He's coming at three.' She said, making herself say it, 'Would you like to be here then?'

'No, thanks. It's your affair. Tell me about it when you come tonight.'

Gerry Prosser, when he arrived, impressed her immediately. His manner indicated that he was as capable of dealing with people as horses. She remembered Paddy cursing Kevin, who he said was no use if he put his foot out of a loose box.

They walked round the yard together and he took it all in without saying much, although she thought how Paddy's influence still showed in its spick-and-span appearance and how settled in the landscape the stable block looked, so permanent, so right to the eye.

'You've only got two horses in?' he said.

'Yes, that's deliberate. I've let it run down because Liam was leaving and I hadn't anyone in his place. He's mid-career at the moment.' She liked the sound of that.

'A personable young man. He knew what he was talking about. Quite a loss, I should think.'

You have no idea, she thought.

She gave him tea in the drawing room and she imagined that impressed him more than the half-empty yard.

'It reminds me of Mr Richardson's place where I worked. We had quite a nice cottage on the grounds but my wife and I divorced. That and the fact that he was retiring made my future uncertain. I decided to come to Dublin and have a look around.'

'Were you thinking of buying?'

'I was uncertain. Principally I needed to move after the divorce.' He looked away. He wasn't going to elaborate.

'I'm taking my time about selling,' Nora told him. 'Would you be interested in a three months' trial on either side?'

'There's not a lot wrong with that. Yes, I would.'

'It's important for me that if I sell, it's to the right person. Paddy built up a good reputation for Marchmount.'

She had already decided that he would do. He didn't talk too much. He was decisive. And although no one would ever have the charm of Paddy, he was likeable and even Paddy's age.

'There's a small flat above the stable block you could have.'

'I might think of that. I have a girlfriend with me. She would like a job too if there was one going.'

'If we took on more horses, we'll need more help in the yard.'

'That's her forte, but she's good in the office too.'

Nora wondered if the girlfriend had been the cause of the divorce. Well, that was no business of hers. It didn't alter the fact that she thought he was right for the job and that Paddy would have endorsed that. He had liked men of the world, someone he could share a joke with. He would be a good representative at race meetings, relieve her of the necessity of following them since she would be in Dublin at Trinity every day.

And what she liked most about him was that his attitude to her was impeccable: no side-glances, leery looks, no gender

201

thing. He was strictly business-like, treating her as a pro-spective employer.

'I know a few owners around here,' he said. 'I used to come over with Mr Richardson's horses. The sooner you add to your two already here the better. Could I see them in the paddock before I go?'

'Sure.' He didn't waste time.

He chose which one of the two he would ride and Sammy mounted the other one and followed him into the paddock. Nora stayed at the fence watching as Gerry Prosser put his horse through its paces. She noticed that from time to time he spoke to Sammy, seemingly asking questions. She admired his easy seat, there was nothing hurried or anxious about him. The horse seemed to respond to his handling. He rode back to her and dismounted, holding the bridle as he patted the horse on the nose.

'This one's showing a bit of promise.'

'Yes, I thought so too. The other one's going to stud, or at least that's what the owner's hoping. So you think the piebald mare's good?'

'Could be. She's a bit flighty but that's because she's not being ridden enough. When she's been worked on, I'd try her at one of the smaller race courses. But we must increase your stable. If you wanted me to come, I could do a bit of discreet advertising.'

She said she wanted him to come. He had all the attributes the other ones hadn't. He seemed competent, and she felt that Liam already liked him. It was the first time in her thinking that she had substituted Liam for Paddy.

Nora was in high spirits when she drove over to Lisbor-ough.

Her mother kissed her when she arrived, saying, 'I'm getting used to having a daughter again.'

'Do you like it?'

'Very much, especially one like you. You're absolutely radiating, did you know that?'

Nora blushed slightly, unusual for her.

'Come along to the drawing room while I prepare some drinks. We'll have them with your grandfather. I told you he's in bed.'

'Yes. I'd love to see him.' Hers was the kind of happiness she wanted to share with everyone.

Colonel Maguire was sitting up in bed listening to the racing results. He looked up when they came in.

'Nice to see you, Nora. Do you remember how Paddy and I used to listen to the results over at Marchmount and then discuss them during dinner?'

'Yes, I certainly do. We're having a gin and vermouth before we eat, Grandfather. We've brought you one.' She was carrying two glasses and handed one to him. 'Try that.'

He took it and sipped. 'Yes, the right amount.' He nodded, pleased, his little moustache quivering.

'Mother mixed it.'

'Thank you, Laure.' He raised his glass to her.

'Cecilia will bring your dinner up on a tray.'

She came in at that moment. 'Well, Colonel Maguire,' she stood with folded arms, 'you've company now all right, your daughter and your granddaughter no less. My, will you look at the eyes on her!' She had glanced in Nora's direction. 'Drinking again! Well, I don't know what the doctor will say about that. You can have a nice piece of lamb, or a fresh-caught fish would be better for you.'

'No, thanks,' Colonel Maguire said. 'I'm fed up to the teeth with Brian's trout. He keeps it in the stables all day before he hands it into the kitchen and it reeks of dung!'

'Now, now, Colonel, you shouldn't look a gift horse in the mouth. Well, how about a nice piece of lamb then straight from the slaughterhouse . . .'

He held up his hand. 'Lamb, please, and with fresh peas and mint out of the garden.'

'Mint sauce it is sure and you've read Maureen's mind. Brian picked—'

'Leave Brian out of it. Give him the fish he caught to take home.'

'Well, he's got plenty of mouths to feed there. You don't have to guess what he does with his spare time . . .' She cast her eyes to the ceiling before she went out chuckling.

'What a woman!' Laure said. 'But she's right about your eyes, Nora. They're as bright as a full moon, aren't they, Daddy?'

'Yes, he said, not looking. 'Damn, I forgot to tell her to cut that white lardy stuff off.'

'Fat. She'll do that.'

Nora had subdued her blush. 'I've got good news. Maybe that's the reason for my eyes. Sit down, Mother, and I'll tell you.'

Laure sat down on the bed. Nora took the chair beside it.

"You listen too, Grandfather. Liam told me of a man who might be interested in Marchmount and he came today. He liked it. He didn't say much, but I could see him appraising it with his eyes. It looked lovely today: the ivy on the clock tower, the paddock and the sloping fields beyond that . . . He's willing to work for me on a three month trial, and after that, we'll see.' Her mother looked pleased.

'Well, that's just fine. It leaves you with a loophole.'

'Ideal,' the colonel said, suddenly on the ball. 'There's no saying what might come out of it but you're not tied down.'

'It was Liam who knew of him,' she said.

'Yes, you said that.' Her mother's look was knowing. 'Has he gone?'

'Yes, this morning.' She turned her head and gazed

through the window at the extent of the Lisborough grounds, in case they should notice her eyes again.

'There must be some snags,' Colonel Maguire said. 'It sounds too good.'

'It's not really a snag, but he mentioned a woman . . .'

'A camp follower?' He bristled.

'Well . . .' Nora smiled. 'He told me he'd got divorced. His owner was selling up and I wondered why he hadn't thought of buying a place he knew. Maybe he wanted to clear out because of the split-up with his wife. He said the girl was with him.'

'Oh, you don't want that!' His moustache went up and down in an agitated fashion. 'Camp followers!' He said it again. 'Camp followers! I would have none of them. I used to tell my men to leave the ladies at home. "You're here to fight," I'd tell them, "not to . . ." ' He took a sip from his glass, his eyes looking regretful.

'Actually, it's a good thing,' Laure said. 'He won't be chasing after girls, even you. Remember Kevin?' She smiled to herself. 'Although that *was* the other way round.'

Grandfather had missed that one, Nora saw. He was sitting with a far-away look in his face, thinking of camp followers.

'Perhaps you could find a job for her as well?' her mother said.

'He suggested that. She worked with him before and she's good in the office, he says.'

'And elsewhere, it would seem. Could you find somewhere for her?'

'Well, if I'm studying she could do the books. That was always my job.'

'Oh, yes, your studying.' She saw her mother thought her studying wasn't to be taken seriously. 'Well, I'd say this man and his girlfriend must have been sent to you from heaven.

Or was it Liam? What do you say, Daddy?' She avoided Nora's eyes.

'What-what? What-what? Who are we talking about?'

'A man who came to see about Marchmount, Grandfather,' Nora said. 'He's called Gerry Prosser. About Paddy's age. Personable. That's what he said about Liam too . . .' She stopped the silly smile from starting.

Cecilia kicked open the door in her usual fashion, bearing a tray. She was as bad as Costain, Nora thought, who left scratches every time he came in or out.

'Now, Colonel.' Cecilia banged down the tray on his knees. 'Here's a fine piece of lamb with the fat cut off, some garden peas and a little jug of mint sauce. My God, some man in the streets of Dublin would be slavering after this.' She smacked her lips.

'Thank you, Cecilia,' Laure said. 'That's just grand. And I see you've brought him a glass of wine.'

'Now, what would the poor old gentleman be without his glass of claret, I'm asking you. You two get away downstairs and tuck into yours before it's spoiled.'

'Yes, on you go, girls,' the colonel said, his eyes on the tray.

Twenty-Four

'He likes attention,' Nora said when she and her mother were downstairs in the dining room.

'Who doesn't? I think he was feeling neglected because of feeling old. It's all right when you can prance about. Well, I know from Norman. He was a very active man, liked his game of golf when he was at home, travelled a great deal. He was, still is, convivial. But it's difficult to be convivial when in the middle of pouring out drinks for a few friends you suddenly fall down on the carpet. That's how it started. And then bit by bit your independence is taken away from you. It takes great fortitude to bear it. I know from watching him, at first with impatience, sometimes with anger, until you realize that the only thing that's going to make the situation bearable is love.'

'You surprise me. Should I tell you that? I thought of you always as selfish, given to tantrums. I do remember the sweetness too, don't worry!' She smiled at her mother. 'But philosophical, never.'

'Norman's changed me. Educated me. He's so wise. We read a lot together – at least I read to him – books which he has to explain to me. It's not the future I imagined for myself, but, there it is. You couldn't turn your back on a man like Norman.'

'I can see that.' She thought of Liam, his vitality, his suppleness, his rightness. So well put together. And his father only four feet ten . . . Life played funny tricks. But that was only Liam's outward appearance, which would fade as time passed. Would she be able to find the real virtues in him as her mother had found in Norman Dexter? All she could say at this moment was that he had a rightness. That was good enough for her. Her mother was speaking.

'My father isn't like Norman. He's becoming senile, and he just needs someone to complain to, who will spoil him a bit. He's a baby. I'm expecting you to stand in for me when I go back. When you think of it, you had quite a selfish life with Paddy compared with some.'

'That's true. Autocratic. A Bouchier trait!' She laughed at her mother. 'Yes, I'll stand in for you, don't you fear. I feel today as if I could spoil the whole world!' She laughed again. 'Mind you, I'm not feeling so guilty about Grandfather. He was all right most of the time, able to go about, to ride, to entertain, and be entertained, mostly regimental dinners, up to a year ago. I think he missed his contacts with the Guards. He dwindled when that had to go. But he and Paddy were good friends. I think it hit him badly when he died.'

'Everybody liked Paddy. God knows.'

The door opened and Maureen came in, a dark young woman with a purposeful air about her. 'How did the lamb go, then, Mrs Dexter?'

'It went very well, Maureen.'

Nora added her praise. 'Really tender, Maureen. I imagine the poor little thing had been skipping about the fields not so long ago. I wish I had someone like you at Marchmount.'

'Yes, Mhairi's gone to the ould uncle. But I'm happy here, catering for the colonel. Cecilia isn't a great hand in the kitchen sure enough but then we don't all have the gift.'

'She looked after me when I was a girl here.' Laure went to her defence.

'To each her own. Hers is the nursing skills. Well, then,

you'll remember the ould days here, Mrs Dexter, before my time . . .' She folded her arms, ready for a crack. 'Yes, Cecilia and I have got the house in good shape between us. You need have no fear.'

'That's music to my ears, Maureen.' Laure became a Bouchier. 'We'll take our coffee in the drawing room, thank you. We'll move there now so you can clear the table.'

'Right-oh!' Maureen looked regretful. 'Well, on you two go to the drawing room and I'll bring in the tray. I'm glad you liked the lamb, though.' She went smartly out of the room.

'Ireland must be the only country where the servants think they should have a crack with you after every course,' Laure said. 'But we have a find in Maureen.'

'Maybe she'll get married and go off?'

'No, she's a widow, believe it or not. I think she's here to stay.'

'What happened to her husband?'

'Shot in Belfast. They lived there. He was in the IRA. Need I say more?'

'Sad, sad . . .'

They settled themselves in the drawing room where there was a bright fire burning, although it was only late summer. A much grander room than their own, Nora always thought. Perhaps the Maguires had been there for ever. She had never wondered about that before, but there were some fine pieces of Georgian furniture and the hangings were rich. There was the Bouchier connection, of course.

'I'm curious about Robbie,' Nora said. 'I had only one close friend at Ste-Catherine's, Antoinette Reynaud, but she came from the south and I never saw her again after we left. Actually, I left earlier than her because I came home to find Paddy ill so I took myself away.'

'He had a grip on you,' her mother said. She sounded

bitter, then maybe she had cause. 'Yes, Robbie and I were close friends. She used to come with me to my grandparents' apartment in the Rue Ste-Honore, and she loved that. She wasn't a flirt, though, like me. She had a boyfriend back home in Boston and it had always been understood that they'd get married when she finished her education. It's not true that the French arrange marriages, at least not more than in other conventional countries, and there were some old Irish Catholic families in Boston. The date for her wedding was actually fixed.'

'She sounds as if she were very biddable.'

'She was. Protected. And then I took her to Chantilly for a day at the races. Paddy had written to invite us. We had been friends since we were point-to-pointing.'

'A day at the races.' Nora echoed the words. She had gone in June to please Paddy, a promise she had made to him, and, thinking of it now, the whole day had a magical quality, hardly real. She could close her eyes at this moment and think of those people chance had gathered together for that day: the two young women in their balloon skirts and high, unsuitable heels, so full of joy; the dignified Mrs Trant and her devious unhappy son who thought he could find that happiness, or forgetfulness, by subjugating women. How evocative that day had been! And there was the young courier, so innocent, but eager for his own kind of happiness, the birth of his first child. Only the truly innocent find real happiness, she thought.

'Did you ever wonder if Paddy had raped Robbie?' she said and was appalled as she listened to the words she was saying.

'Raped!' Laure looked mystified, not shocked at the suggestion, but at Nora herself. 'Whatever makes you think that?'

'Coincidence in a way. Because I had what you might call

an unpleasant experience when I was staying at Le Manoir. I
had met this man at Chantilly, and he came to Chartres, and
I foolishly invited him back, and he tried to rape me. I was
saved by Robbie's son hammering on the door. He had heard
me screaming for help.'

'What an extraordinary thing!' Her mother blew out her
breath. 'Here was I thinking I was going to discover an
innocent little daughter and she talks about rape as if it was a
walk in the park.'

'You can get raped there too.' They both burst out laughing, more at the sheer audacity of the conversation, or was it
a bridge they had crossed so that they could discuss anything
at all?

'I can laugh now,' Nora said, wiping her eyes, 'but I can
tell you that man put the fear of God in me! I was so innocent
that I hardly knew what I was holding on to, but I was as sure
as God not going to let him have it!' They were away again,
helpless.

'Oh, dear, oh, dear,' Laure said at last. 'Laughter has a
great effect on all the old prejudices. No, I'm pretty sure
Paddy didn't rape Robbie. It was the game of seduction he
liked. Power. Exercising his maleness. He could be quite
irresistible. Robbie was a very repressed girl. Because of her
parents and Bob Clancy, she had never had a chance to have
any experience. You don't miss what you've never had.

'The future was all that mattered to her, getting married,
having children, and then the seducer, Paddy, came along.
Oh, the charm of him! The pretty speeches! The quirk of a
smile. All the trimmings. No, I'm sure he just swept her off
her feet literally and she lost her head, to put it politely. They
had gone back to Le Manoir after the races. I was otherwise
engaged.' She had a quirk of a smile too. 'She was so
ashamed, and yet thrilled to the marrow half the time.
She went around like someone in another world. Didn't

hear you when you spoke to her, and when she did, she burst into fits of weeping.'

'Didn't Paddy try to see her again?'

'Oh, yes. She went back to Boston, but he wrote and wrote, even telephoned. She wouldn't speak to him. She was in the throes of a deep religious guilt, I imagine. She was in her second month of pregnancy when she married Bob. She must have gone through hell keeping a secret like that. Craig was duly born and Bob naturally treated him as his son. The waters had long since closed over the whole affair. I honestly believe that sometimes she doubted if the episode with Paddy had ever happened. She got over him, but he never got over her.'

'Were you back in Lisborough by then?'

'Yes. Twiddling my thumbs. Daddy doing his best. Paddy and I teamed up. At first he used me to pour out his grief about Robbie ditching him, as he thought, but he gradually got over it. One evening when we were on a slight bender together he said, "Why don't we get married?" and I said, "Why not?" That was in 1964 and you were born two years later. I'd had one or two miscarriages before that. The Bouchiers are bad breeders.'

'Weren't you happy for a little?' In her own happiness she could have wept for this unhappy woman.

'Not for long. Do you know, I sometimes think if he had been able to marry Robbie, their marriage would have turned out just like ours. There's nothing like "what might have been" to keep the flame burning. He bashed his head against that brick wall all the time, only assuaged by frequent encounters or *re-enactements* with the opposite sex.'

'And then you went off with Kevin Flannagan?'

'Yes. Anyone would have done. I hope you never know the sense of failure in an unhappy marriage.' Laure stubbed out her cigarette. The ashtray was full. 'So that's the sad tale of Paddy. And me.'

'Yes, it's sad. I hope it's not like that with me and Liam.'

'So it's you and Liam, is it?'

'Yes, unlike Robbie, but quite like you with Paddy, a slow, nurturing process.'

'Ah, but you'll be first in Liam's heart.'

'Do you think there was a curse on Le Manoir? Blanche, Robbie and then me – nearly but not quite?'

'Don't give me any of that Irish will o' the wisp nonsense. It was burned down because it was sitting in the middle of a village which was being fought over. It was just hard luck that my mother had chosen it for her little *dalliance*, shall we say?'

'I don't think you're as hard as you sound.'

'No, I'm not hard. I'm clear-sighted. That's the only thing I hope I've given you. Honesty.'

'I slept with Liam before he left,' Nora said, being honest.

Her mother smiled. 'Tell me something I don't know.'

Twenty-Five

G erry Prosser came with his girlfriend, Anne Baker, a quietly-spoken youngish woman, possibly a few years his junior. Her fairly ordinary appearance was redeemed by fine hazel eyes. They decided Nora, as they must have Gerry (judging by the strong rapport between them), that she was someone to be reckoned with. The hazel eyes spotted the piebald right away.

'That one has promise, Gerry,' she said, and to Nora, 'What's her name?'

'I don't know. We haven't had her long.'

'She's a runner. And elegant with it.' She was watching it being ridden round the paddock by Sammy. 'How would Café Crème suit?'

'I like it,' Nora said. 'Elegant. She might run at Chantilly sometime.'

When they were inside having coffee, Anne Baker said to Nora, 'You have a lovely place here.'

'I've been singing its praises to her,' Gerry said. 'And I've good news for you, Miss Malone.'

'Nora.'

'OK. I've got the promise of two horses for your stables. I've brought all the details.' He produced some documents from a briefcase he was carrying.

'We'll go over them later.' She turned to Anne Baker as she said, 'If I increase my stables, would you like to work here?'

214

'I'll do it for nothing provided you don't mind me sharing Gerry's flat?' She had a good smile too, an older smile, a woman of her time.

'I've no objection. Suppose we make you general factotum, looking after the books, keeping an eye on the yard. I generally do it but I'm going to be rather busy.'

'So I believe. I would try to make myself useful. Let's say payment to be arranged.'

'Suits me.' Nora had a feeling they both understood each other. Although Anne Baker wasn't a chatterer, she was frank.

'I'm divorced, like Gerry. I have a nineteen-year-old son in a yard at Newmarket. My former husband was a trainer.'

'Yes? So was my father.'

Anne smiled; a disarming smile.

I'm going to like her, Nora thought. It had been a satisfactory morning.

She had been right to trust them. In another month they had five horses in the stables, Gerry and Anne were installed in the flat and the place was running like clockwork. And Gerry was liked by the lads. They would work well for him.

Laure was going back to Arizona. She'd had disquietening news from the nurse. Norman had been moved to hospital, and although he wasn't complaining, the nurse thought she should come back. She had her ticket booked and was leaving the following morning when Nora went to Lisborough, which she did several times each week now.

'You're right to go back, Mother,' she said. 'Don't worry about Grandfather. I'll see that he doesn't get into mischief.'

The colonel was there and he laughed derisively. 'Not much chance for that nowadays. But I'll miss you, Laure.'

'You're going to have a lovely, happy young woman at your beck and call. What more could you want?'

'I wouldn't mind being with my regiment again, even at

Dunkirk, and that's saying something. And having my dear Blanche here.' His moustache quivered, his eyes watered with the lability of the old. 'Sometimes when I look back . . .'

'Now, now, Daddy,' Laure said, 'you'll have us all crying. Let's go into the dining room and see what Maureen has cooked up for my farewell feast.'

He brightened immediately.

Maureen had game. 'Done to a turn,' she said, poking the birds on their salver. 'Did you ever see a brace of grouse more beautiful than those two lying there? And that gravy, Co-lonel! Go easy, because there's so much red wine in it, that it'll have you reeling!'

'Where are the vegetables, Maureen?' Laure asked, stopping her in mid-flow.

'Right behind you on the sideboard, Mrs Dexter.' The two tureens descended in a wide arc onto the table. 'Game chips and little roast potatoes and celery as white as a shroud in its cinnamon sauce and cabbage mashed to bits in farm butter till it's as smooth as silk. It's a banquet this, not an ordinary dinner.'

'You should be writing for the *Irish Times*,' Laure said, smiling. 'How about bringing in the plates?'

'I forgot the . . .? Well, it's not to be wondered at, carried away as I am by the beauty of this repast! Do you hear me, *repast*! Now where did I get such a word. I must have swallowed the dictionary.'

'On you go, Maureen,' the colonel said.

She went, giving him what had to be called, Nora thought, the glad eye.

The next morning she drove her mother to the airport. 'Don't worry about Grandfather,' she said. 'I'll keep an eye on him. I've grown very fond of him.' She smiled in the mirror.

'Yes, he's an endearing old soul. I'll miss him. Things are going well for you at Marchmount?'

'Couldn't be better. Gerry is doing well and bringing in new horses, he and Anne seem very happy. She's an asset. I'm pretty sure he'll buy at the end of the three months.'

'And you're pretty sure you'll sell?'

'I'll talk it over with Liam. He'll be home soon.'

'Is he still the one?'

She nodded, feeling her face light up and trying to dowse it like a candle.

She hugged her mother before she joined the queue. 'I'm going to miss you.' The tears came. 'I'm really too old to behave like this. I should have grown out of mothers.'

'Well, we've a lot of leeway to make up. And I'll tell you this, I go away with a good heart. Daddy's better and I've never seen a girl who looked happier.'

'What did I tell you? A girl's best friend is her mother. On you go. My love to your Norman, and don't disappear like that again.'

She watched Laure going through the barrier. She had style. The ticket collector was smiling at her in her loden green cloak. Yes, you would have said she was a woman of quality.

She was sad and happy driving back to Marchmount. Everything looked so good. She had a mother she could be proud of, and Liam whom she was proud of, and Marchmount was in good hands, and at last she felt she had grown up to meet her age, which was an entirely satisfactory feeling.

She telephoned Liam when she got home. 'I've just seen my mother off for Arizona. Her husband needs her. I don't need her but I'm proud of her and I love her. I'm very happy. When are you coming home?'

'Very soon.' And then they indulged in a conversation which they were both ashamed of, but which made her happier still. He would be home in a fortnight. She didn't deserve such luck. Everything had come together.

In a few days she heard from her mother. Although Norman had been ill enough to be removed to hospital, his pleasure in seeing her had bucked him up quite a bit. Happiness swelled up inside Nora. It couldn't get better.

On the day before she would go to the airport to meet Liam, she drove over to Lisborough for her regular Sunday visit. The colonel liked her to come to lunch. He looked well, and they went for their usual Sunday stroll in the grounds before they ate.

'You'll have to come over and meet my new manager, Grandfather,' she said. 'You'd be pleased at the way he's licking the place into shape. We have five horses now and they're working on a filly which they're hoping to race soon. We've called her Café Crème. It was Anne's idea, his girl-friend.' He didn't say 'camp follower' this time.

'Where did she get the name from?'

'From the filly's colouring. She's a piebald.'

'I'd like to see her. You can drive me over when I'm feeling better.'

She smiled at that. 'Yes, of course, Grandfather. When you're feeling up to it,' Laure had said to spoil the old codger a bit.

'The trees are beginning to turn,' she said, as they walked through the copse.

'Yes, a sad time for old people. Thank goodness the beech near the house keeps its leaves for a bit.'

'It's worth waiting for. That glorious colour. We used to have a huge bunch of them on the hall table. If you put the stems in glycerine they lasted all winter. That was Paddy's tip.'

Add a huge vase of beech leaves to your mental picture, she thought. The hall fire with its red heart and she and Paddy sitting in front of it had only a gentle resonance in her mind now.

'Look at that tree,' her grandfather said, pointing with his stick. 'That trick of the leaves . . . it looks silver from here.'

She looked and the shimmer of leaves made her feel dizzy. Her head swam; they were shimmering rhythmically and she had a feeling of nausea in the pit of her stomach. She stopped walking.

'What's wrong, eh?' the colonel said testily. 'We haven't gone nearly far enough. We always come out—'

'I suddenly feel a bit funny . . .'

'It's that ridiculous running into Dublin to those classes. Surely you've enough to do . . .'

She was breathing steadily, willing the dizziness to go. She looked away from the aspen and she felt her head clearing. She turned back, relieved.

'I'm perfectly all right now. The leaves looked like crinkled tinfoil. I could almost hear them rattling. Stupid.' She took another deep breath. 'Yes, I'm all right. Let's walk on.' Walk on, walk on . . . that's what you say to Starlight. Steady on, Nora . . .

'No, I think I've gone far enough.' He was petulant. Or was he? 'Let's go back and have a drink. Brandy's good if you feel squeamish.'

'All right, Grandfather.' She took his arm. It had been a trick of her eyes.

She kept the little trick of her eyes from Liam the next day when she met him at the airport. She waited until they were in bed.

'You certainly upset the apple cart,' she said when he was leaning over her as she lay smiling.

'Do you mean now?' He looked pleased.

'No, the last time. The first time. I'm pregnant.'

He stared at her.

'I've been to the doctor. He confirms it.'

He was struck dumb. 'God in heaven!' he said at last,

219

looking pleased. 'I didn't know I was that good. What are you going to do?'

'Do? I'm going to phone my mother. It's the daughterly thing to do.'

'Then we'll get married.'

'Then we'll get married.'

He looked judicious. 'Marchmount's a decent place to bring up children.'

'But not necessarily to make it our life's work. There are my studies.'

'And my job. There's another project ahead. Brazil.'

'And there are working mothers.'

'And you've got a first-rate trainer.'

'Who might want to buy Marchmount.'

'Decisions, decisions.'

'All those delightful decisions.' She sighed happily. 'Lie down, Liam. You'll get a crick in your neck.'

He lay down.